JOSS WOOD

RECKLESS ENVY

P9-CPX-541

HARLEQUIN
DESIRE

Special thanks and acknowledgment are
given to Joss Wood for her contribution to the
Dynasties: Seven Sins miniseries.

Recycling programs
for this product may
not exist in your area.

ISBN-13: 978-1-335-20932-0

Reckless Envy

Copyright © 2020 by Harlequin Books S.A.

This edition published by arrangement with Harlequin Books S.A.

For questions and comments about the quality of this book,
please contact us at CustomerService@Harlequin.com.

Harlequin Enterprises ULC
22 Adelaide St. West, 40th Floor
Toronto, Ontario M5H 4E3, Canada
www.Harlequin.com

Printed in U.S.A.

DYNASTIES

_SN_

Seven Sins

One man's betrayal can destroy generations.

Fifteen years ago, a hedge-fund hotshot vanished with billions, leaving the high-powered families of Falling Brook changed forever.

Now seven heirs, shaped by his betrayal, must reckon with the sins of the past.

Passion may be their only path to redemption.

Experience all Seven Sins!

* * *

Ruthless Pride by **Naima Simone**

This CEO's pride led him to give up his dreams for his family. Now he's drawn to the woman who threatens everything...

Forbidden Lust by **Karen Booth**

He's always resisted his lust for his best friend's sister—until they're stranded together in paradise...

Insatiable Hunger by **Yahrah St. John**

His unbridled appetite for his closest friend is unleashed when he believes she's fallen for the wrong man...

Hidden Ambition by **Jules Bennett**

Ambition has taken him far, but revenge could cost him his one chance at love...

Reckless Envy by **Joss Wood**

When this shark in the boardroom meets the one woman he can't have, envy takes over...

Untamed Passion by **Cat Schield**

Will this black sheep's self-destructive wrath flame out when he's expecting an heir of his own?

Slow Burn by **Janice Maynard**

If he's really the idle playboy his family claims, will his inaction threaten a reunion with the woman who got away?

"What do you want, Velez?"

You. Naked. As soon as possible.

Matt ran his hand through his hair as he turned to face Emily. "Why are you wearing that ridiculously big ring? Why are you really marrying Morris, Emily? And don't tell me it's because you love him."

"Maybe I do."

"BS."

When he got out of his head, pushed aside his envy and jealousy—and his need to have her—he still, instinctively, had the feeling her engagement was a sham. "Are you in trouble?" he demanded, his voice rough.

"No, I'm not in trouble, Velez. And even if I was, why would I confide in you?" Emily asked, tipping her head to the side. "I'm just another girl who threw herself at you, one of the few you didn't bother to catch."

He would never tell her that he'd been so tempted to start something meaningful with her...

* * *

Reckless Envy by Joss Wood is part of the Dynasties: Seven Sins series.

Dear Reader,

I am so thrilled to be part of this dynamic series with the other brilliant Harlequin Desire authors.

Emily Arnott's father lost millions in the Black Crescent debacle, and her mother left them shortly afterward. Her father set about rebuilding his company, and Emily was left to raise herself and her brother.

Emily now works with her dad and is considered a Falling Brook "good girl," someone who doesn't put a foot out of line. Well, she tried a decade ago but bad boy Matt Velez refused her New Year's Eve advances. They've avoided each other ever since.

But life is about to get complicated for both Matt and Emily: Matt is interviewing for the position of Black Crescent CEO and Emily is being blackmailed into marriage...

Matt knows that there is something very wrong with Emily's engagement, and he's determined to stop it, initially because he will do anything to thwart his archenemy, Emily's fiancé. And then because he realizes that Emily might, just might, be his forever person...

They say the course of true love never runs smoothly, but this is one wild ride!

Happy reading!

Joss

Xxx

Connect with me on Facebook (JossWoodAuthor), Twitter (@JossWoodbooks), BookBub (Joss-Wood) or my website (JossWoodBooks.com).

Joss Wood loves books and traveling—especially to the wild places of southern Africa and, well, anywhere. She's a wife, a mom to two teenagers and slave to two cats. After a career in local economic development, she now writes full-time. Joss is a member of Romance Writers of America and Romance Writers of South Africa.

Books by Joss Wood

Harlequin Desire

Murphy International

One Little Indiscretion
Temptation at His Door
Back in His Ex's Bed

Love in Boston

Friendship on Fire
Hot Christmas Kisses
The Rival's Heir
Second Chance Temptation

Dynasties: Seven Sins

Reckless Envy

Visit her Author Profile page at Harlequin.com, or josswoodbooks.com, for more titles.

You can also find Joss Wood on Facebook, along with other Harlequin Desire authors, at Facebook.com/harlequindesireauthors!

Prologue

Six years ago...

Emily Arnott tossed a glass of champagne down her throat and scowled at the massive glitter ball hanging from the ceiling of the overly decorated ballroom of the Falling Brook Country Club.

Three, two, one…

Happy damn New Year to me.

Lodged in the corner of the room, Emily blinked back tears and wished she was anywhere but here. It had been Gina's idea to attend this party at the exclusive country club situated on the outskirts of her hometown of Falling Brook as the club was the gathering place for the wealthy residents of the area.

Emily's father had purchased tickets for the much-anticipated ball but, because he hated crowds and people, he'd passed the tickets on to her. As far as Emily could tell, her best friend and college room-mate was having a blast. Gina was slow dancing with someone she vaguely recognized, Drew something, and they'd just exchanged a kiss hot enough to strip the expensive paper from the walls of the ballroom.

Gina was going to score tonight while Emily was…not.

Emily closed her eyes and banged the back of her head against the wall, feeling heat creeping up her neck and flowing into her cheeks. Unlike Gina, the move she'd made had not resulted in starting the new year off with a bang or even, sadly, with a mild grope or even a kiss.

No, she'd just been swatted away like an annoying fly.

Emily felt feminine hands on her shoulders and she opened her eyes as Gina drew her into a hug. "Happy New Year, Em. Isn't this the most fantastic party?"

Uh, that would be a no.

Emily, not wanting to spoil Gina's evening, just handed her a pained smile and took a sip from her glass of champagne.

Gina took one look at her face and grimaced. "What happened?"

Emily gestured to Gina's date. "I'll tell you about it tomorrow. Drew is looking for you."

Gina tossed her hair. "He'll wait," she stated with all the confidence of an Italian starlet with more curves than an S-bend. "Why are you standing in the corner looking like you just swallowed a bucket of fire ants?"

As well as being gorgeous, Gina was also persistent. "I swung and struck out," Emily reluctantly admitted.

"It happens," Gina philosophically replied.

Emily knew that it rarely, if ever, happened to her sexy friend.

"What happened, honey?" Gina gently asked her.

Emily sighed and raised her champagne glass. "Aided by a couple of glasses of Dutch courage, I thought I'd have a one-night stand, a little fling."

"It's your twenty-first in a couple of days—it's allowed. And God knows, you deserve some fun."

Gina was the most nonjudgmental person Emily knew and that was only one of the reasons she loved her. "Well, admittedly, I aimed a bit high and made a move on Matt Velez—"

Gina looked around, a tiny frown between her dramatic dark brows. "Who?"

Emily glanced around but didn't spot Falling Brook's ex–bad boy and MJR Investing's wunderkind and their youngest-appointed CEO. If she was really lucky, he would've left the party and she could stop skulking in the corner. No, she couldn't spot him and she was glad because every time she laid eyes on the olive-skinned, dark-eyed, square-jawed and ripped-as-hell Antonio Banderas look-alike, her IQ dropped a hundred points.

With his slightly crooked nose, Matt wasn't pretty per se. But something about his rough angles-and-planes face and enigmatic dark eyes made her breath hitch and her stomach swirl. She was tired of college boys and Matteo Velez was very much a *man*, masculine from the top of his wavy dark hair to his big feet, radiating vitality and complete confidence as he moved through the well-dressed, sophisticated and moneyed crowd.

Every woman in the room, from eighty down, gave him a second, or third, look. Emily knew he just had to crook his finger and any one of them would come running. No wonder he hadn't reacted when, having found herself standing next to him at the bar, she had asked whether she could buy him a drink.

Drinks are included in the price of the ticket, honey, he'd told her, sounding disinterested.

Ah, yeah, right. Um, I'm Em... Emily.

Matt. He'd taken the hand she'd held out, given it a quick shake and quickly dropped it like she'd had a particularly contagious disease.

Gina was always telling her to be up-front, that men liked straightforward women, so she'd searched for something to say that fell between *God, you're hot* and *Please kiss me*.

He'd been about to walk away so Emily had racked her brain for something intelligent, or witty, to say in order to hold his attention.

Kiss me if I'm wrong, but dinosaurs still exist, right? Emily had mentally slapped her hand against her forehead, not quite able to believe that she'd said something so cheesy. Matt had looked as astonished as she'd felt.

Are you hitting on me? he'd demanded, cocoa-colored eyes flashing. And not with lust. Annoyance, maybe.

Um...yeah?

You're really bad at it. He'd glanced at the glass of champagne in her hand. *Are you drunk?*

Tipsy maybe, Emily had reluctantly admitted. She hadn't been, not really, but admitting to being drunk was better than saying he was making her feel nervous and very much out of her depth.

Matt had caught the attention of the barman, ordered a glass of water and shoved it into her hand. *Drink this and go home. You're a guppy in a room full of sharks and you're going to get eaten up.*

Normally, she would have been halfway across the room by then, but something about Matt had kept her feet glued to the floor. She was striking out but she'd thought she'd give it one last shot. *I'm not looking for anything more than a fun way to see in the New Year.*

Matt's sensual mouth had thinned. *Emily, it is Emily, right?* When she'd nodded, he'd sighed and stepped back. *Apart from being too young for me, you're drunk.*

Tipsy maybe and I'll be twenty-one in a few days, Emily had babbled, knowing soil was flying over her shoulder from the ridiculously deep hole she was digging.

Just like she wasn't enough for her mother, she wasn't enough for Matt Velez either. When would she ever learn? And why weren't her feet taking orders from her brain and walking her away?

Matt had groaned and dug his fingers into his

eye sockets. *Why do they let infants into parties like these?* He'd dropped his hand and his eyes had slammed into hers. *Okay, let me put this another way...you're most definitely not my type.*

Emily finished telling Gina her story and watched as sympathy replaced horror on Gina's face. She knew her friend was holding back an enormous wince. "Oh, God, Em, you are so bad at picking up guys."

She couldn't argue with her statement. "Tell me about it. I need lessons—"

Emily's words drifted off as she caught a glimpse of Matt Velez slow dancing across the room, his arms around a woman with pale blond hair and wearing a black dress.

Emily picked up a curl off her breast—yep, still blond—and looked down at her tight-fitting cocktail dress. It hadn't changed color either; it was still black.

Not his type, huh? So why was he dancing with someone—his lips against her temple, his hand low on her butt—who looked a lot like her? Emily reached back and placed her hand against the cool wall, looking for something to steady her. There was a close resemblance between her and the woman in Matt's arms but, yet again, she'd been rejected for some strange reason she couldn't comprehend.

Gina gave her a commiserating smile, squeezed her arm and joined Drew on the dance floor. Standing against the wall, Emily glared at Matt's back and raked her hands through her long hair. She saw the worried look Gina sent her and returned a reassuring smile. She was fine, and even if she wasn't, there was nothing Gina could do to change the situation.

Unlike her, Gina grew up with two parents who thought the sun rose and set with her and told her, with great enthusiasm and conviction, that she could be and do anything and that she was loved beyond measure. Emily was a stranger to that sort of love and support: her dad, she supposed, loved her but lived, mostly, in his own world, and her mom bailed on her marriage and motherhood when Emily was fourteen. Few people understood, Gina included, that when the person who is supposed to love and care for you the most in this world leaves you—*by choice*—it's difficult to believe anyone and everyone who becomes important to you will not do the same.

Despite being on intimate terms with that truth, Emily'd spent the past seven years chasing validation and acceptance, her need for connection greater than her fear of being rejected. Despite knowing it would never happen, she was still waiting for her mom to reach out and acknowledge her, for her dad to step out of his solitary world and recognize that she needed him to be, well, her dad.

Three years into college and she still looked for praise from her professors, threw herself at any boy who gave her the littlest bit of attention, and she was overly invested and frequently clingy in her relationships with her girlfriends.

She was, Emily ruefully admitted, a basket case.

And worse than that, she was humiliating herself and she was done. It was time to stop looking for the good opinion and validation of others. As the old year rolled into the new, Emily vowed to become as emotionally independent as possible.

She wasn't going to seek validation and acceptance anymore, and from this moment on, her opinion was the only one that counted. From now on she intended to live her life carefully, thoughtfully, being fully on guard for the possibility of being rejected and abandoned again.

New year, new Emily. It was time for her to grow up.

And, by the way, screw you, Matt Velez.

The woman in his arms—God, he couldn't remember her name—was a poor substitute for whom he really wanted to be his dance partner. Her hair, falling over his hand resting between her shoulder blades, was coarse from repeated highlighting, and her scent was spicy and heavy, clogging his nose and throat.

Matt Velez looked over her shoulder to the corner of the room where Emily stood with her back against the wall, and he wished she was in his arms, her slim, toned body pressed up against his, her scent light and fresh, hair soft.

When he'd turned at her softly spoken offer to buy him a drink and looked into her eyes—a deep, dark blue just a shade off violet—his normally unexcitable heart jumped into his throat. With her high cheekbones and creamy skin, she looked like the poster child for Christmas angels, innocent and pure.

Everything Matt wasn't.

He'd almost said yes to her offer, had been on the point of dragging her out of the room and bundling her into his car when he remembered that she was too young, too innocent, too…

Too desirable. *Far* too desirable.

Matt didn't mess with innocents, and even if Emily didn't have a reputation for being Falling Brook's golden girl, any fool could see that she was as wide-eyed and innocent as they came. She was sweet and soft and ridiculously naive and he was pretty sure she'd never had sex before, never mind a one-night stand.

Matt had never been innocent, had more street smarts at ten than she did now and was an expert at one-night stands, brief affairs and flings.

He used to be Falling Brook's bad boy, their best-known rebel, once hated but now feted because he was the CEO of MJR Investing in nearby Manhattan. It always amused Matt that his handful of Falling Brook clients, born with silver spoons in their mouths, blithely pretended he'd never egged their or their friends' houses, taken their expensive cars on unauthorized joyrides and spent hours steaming up said cars with their indulged and pretty daughters.

Their precious princesses had been eager to walk on the wild side and Matt had been happy to be their guide.

But certain girls, even back then, had been off-limits to the likes of him, and Emily Arnott, had she been closer to his age, would've been one of those girls. The Arnotts were, possibly, one of the most respected families in Falling Brook, and the town was super protective of the single father with a special-needs son and angelic-looking daughter. Not only had Leonard's wife left him when he lost the bulk of his fortune in the Black Crescent embezzlement scandal, but she'd—as the gossip went—also cut all ties with her ex and her kids.

Leonard was left to rebuild his company and raise two kids on his own. But soon—the hot gossip even reached Matt's less salubrious side of the tracks—Leonard's main focus became his company and his work and Emily was left to not only raise herself but to look after her brother, as well.

She'd had a rough time and, according to the rumor mill—and yes, his ears perked up every time her name was mentioned—life for the gorgeous blonde was, finally, evening out. Her brother was now a resident of Brook Village, a home for adults with intellectual special needs, and Emily was about to graduate college and was going to join her father's wealth-management firm.

She was a town favorite and she did not need the town's biggest rebel and player—no matter how much he wanted her—messing with her head.

And Matt didn't need her tap-dancing her way through his.

Because something about Emily Arnott intrigued him, fascinated him, and his fascination went beyond some bed-based fun. He had the insane need to find out what was going on behind those luminous eyes, what thoughts were tumbling around her pretty head.

Sure, he wanted to know how she tasted, whether her skin was as smooth and creamy as he suspected, her hair as soft, but images of her being in his life kept bombarding him. Rolling over and seeing her in his bed, early-morning cups of coffee at the breakfast table, curling up on the sofa at night, watching a movie. The normal and the mundane…he instinctively wanted that with her.

But Matt didn't allow himself to want, wouldn't allow himself to dream. Because when he wanted too much, dreamed too hard, life—and his parents—never delivered.

It was easier not to wish or want; that way, he could avoid disappointment.

The woman in his arms pulled away, tipped her head back and handed him a sensual smile. "Do you want to get out of here?"

Matt, his thoughts on Emily, almost said no but caught the words behind his teeth. "A couple of hours, no commitments and no promises?"

She nodded, her hand stroking the lapels of his tuxedo jacket. "If that's the way you want to play it, lover."

With her—and every other woman he met—it was.

Matt, without allowing himself to look at Emily Arnott again, followed her out of the room and into the chilly night air, desperately trying to ignore his raging disappointment that he was leaving with the wrong blonde.

But dreams were for fools, reality was what mattered, and hey, at least he wasn't seeing in the new year alone.

One

Matteo Velez sped up the winding tree-lined road to Falling Brook's country club, enjoying the leashed power of his new, eye-wateringly expensive AMG Roadster. Resisting the temptation to keep driving, he gently touched the brakes. The car instantly responded and he pulled to a smooth stop in front of the valet station. Matt considered parking his brand-new baby himself—he loved this car—but eventually, and reluctantly, dropped the keys and a tip into the open palm of the valet.

"Thank you, sir. I'll take good care of it."

Matt winced, remembering that those were the same words he'd often used when he'd parked cars at this same venue more than twelve, fifteen years ago. He'd been fired after two weeks because he hadn't been able to resist the urge to take a guest's Porsche 911 for a spin. He'd nearly lost control of the car and was grateful he'd only lost his job, not his life. The thought of having a teenager in control of his state-of-the-art, furiously powerful car sent chills up and down his spine.

"Can you drive a stick?"

"Yes, sir."

Matt cocked his head and narrowed his eyes at the young man. Matt watched as he carefully slid into the driver's seat and pulled on his seat belt to make the fifty-yard drive to the parking area. He studied the controls before gently easing the gearshift into gear. He pulled off without grinding the gears and kept his speed just above a fast walking pace. Matt relaxed; this kid was, unlike him, a Boy Scout and wouldn't dream of taking a wild ride in his fast car.

Matt watched his car until it was out of sight before buttoning the jacket on his dark gray designer suit, perfectly content to walk into a swanky fundraiser alone. He was used to operating solo; he'd been doing it most of his life, and this was just another cocktail party and silent auction to raise funds for Falling Brook's independent K-through-12 school. He was pretty sure that the well-funded school wasn't short of money, but flaunt-my-designer-threads fundraisers were an important part of the town's social calendar, somewhere to be seen and to show off how wealthy and generous you were.

It was also a great place to mine the town for gossip, for anything Matt could use to his advantage.

MJR Investing only had a few clients from Falling Brook, but he was always on the lookout for more. It was at functions like these where Matt heard whispers of infidelities, of divorces, of inheritances and of business losses, all of which could influence MJR's clients', or potential clients', stock portfolios. Forewarned was, as the cliché went, forearmed.

Matt stepped into the luxurious lobby of the country club, idly noting that nothing had changed. It was what it was, a place for the great and good of Falling Brook to gather, and membership of the club was harder to obtain than a jaunt around the moon.

To his parents, the Falling Brook Country Club was the height of sophistication and the pinnacle of acceptance, and they'd been over the moon when his brother—the academically brilliant Juan—had been admitted into its hallowed halls just a few months before. They didn't know, or care, that their younger son had been a member for years. Then again, Mama and Papa Velez were all about Juan and his achievements; they hadn't shown much interest in the life of their second son, the family "mistake."

When perfection was handed to you the first time around, why waste time, energy and money on your unwanted second son?

He rarely thought of his estranged parents these days and Matt pushed the memories, and the hurt, away. He glanced at the mirror in front of him and caught the reflection of a woman walking into the lobby, blond hair pulled back, highlighting those magnificent cheekbones and wide, purple-blue eyes. It

would be easy to say that Emily Arnott still looked
like an angel, and with her blond hair and big, round
eyes, and fine features, it was an apt comparison to
make.

And others often had. But to Matt, older now, the oft-
repeated words showed a distinct lack of creativity...

There was no denying that she was beautiful;
she was. Tall, slim, composed. Her dress was floor-
length, a skin-hugging fabric the color of steel, with
a slit parting to display a slim, toned thigh with every
step she took. It was a sexy dress, but Matt knew that
Emily Arnott could wear a garbage bag and he'd still
find her enchanting.

He'd never forgotten her clumsy pass at him so
many years ago and the memory was still farm fresh.
Six years had passed since he'd turned her down and
it was still one of his biggest regrets.

Sure, she'd been too young and a little drunk—
and he'd been rocked to his toes by desire—but he
could've been kinder when he rejected her, or here's
a thought, not rejected her at all. But she'd knocked
him, metaphorically, off his feet—something that
never happened to him—and he'd been so tempted
to take her up on her no-strings offer. But, because
his heart had been jumping out of his chest, his blood
had been rushing south and his world had been shift-
ing and sliding away, he'd slammed on the brakes,
terrified.

A dozen images had flashed through his mind during that brief conversation: her in a simple wedding
dress, his ring on her finger. Blond-haired, dark-eyed

children, those extraordinary eyes dominating a face lined by age and experience. He'd known he'd find her as beautiful at seventy as he did now.

He'd never known love, had never felt like a part of the family he'd been born into and had decided at an early age that he was better off alone, and not before or since had any woman threatened his lone-wolf status. Emily Arnott, in the space of an ultra-brief conversation, had him thinking of weddings and babies and forever.

Jesus.

Nobody but she had ever managed to knock him so badly off-balance and he hadn't cared for the sensation. He'd craved her with a ferocity he'd never felt before. There had been so much he'd wanted as a child, from toys to affection to attention, and slowly, he came to realize that the more he longed for something, the less chance he had of receiving his heart's desire. He didn't *want*. Even as a kid, he'd never allowed passion to sweep him away; he'd made distancing himself into an art form.

If you didn't wish for or expect anything, you never found yourself disenchanted and disillusioned.

But, young and stupid, Emily Arnott had knocked him off his feet. And, because he felt a little—no, a lot—out of control, unhinged and off-kilter, he'd acted like a jerk in his attempt to put as much distance between them as possible. Because, he reluctantly admitted, he'd recognized her as being dangerous…

But he was older now and even more committed to his career and his single life. He wasn't a monk, far from it, but a relationship didn't feature on his list of priorities. And it never would. He didn't allow situations, and definitely not women, to knock him off his stride.

Sure, Emily was still fire hot, and it helped that she, on the very few times she'd acknowledged him since then—either by an arched eyebrow or an I'll-drop-you-where-you-stand look—made it very clear that she had no intention of forgiving his clumsy, jerkish "thanks but no thanks."

Matt moved toward the bank of elevators, conscious of her long-legged stride across the lobby. He pushed the nearest elevator button and inhaled her light, fresh perfume. Three steps, two steps, one...

"Are you going up to the ballroom?" Emily asked, her voice holding a sexy rasp causing the fabric over his crotch area to tighten. He still, dammit, wanted to hear her sexy voice in the dead of night, when they were alone and naked, painting dirty words in the darkness.

Yep, the chemistry and attraction hadn't faded. *Great.*

Matt slowly turned and looked into her purple-blue eyes, noticing the shock and the annoyance. Distaste slid into her eyes but underneath that emotion, something else flashed. "Oh, it's you."

Matt gestured her into the open elevator, followed her inside and pushed the button to take them to the ballroom. When he turned around to face her, her eyes jerked up and Matt arched his eyebrows, pretty sure she'd been checking out his ass.

He gripped the railing behind his back and smiled at her. "Like what you see?"

Emily's cool expression didn't change. "It's a nice package." She shrugged. "But I've grown up—I now like a bit of substance underneath the pretty wrapping paper."

Ouch.

Matt, not the type to back down, opened his mouth to retaliate but quickly swallowed down his hot response. And the urge to kiss her senseless. He hauled in some air and tightened his fingers around the railing, words that normally came easily deserting him.

He needed to break the tense silence but had no idea what to say. He didn't socialize much when he was in Falling Brook, preferring to use his house here as an escape from people and the pressures of working in Manhattan, that intense, fast-moving environment. He'd only encountered Emily three times in six years and he didn't know when he'd next have a chance to get her alone.

He might as well bite the bullet and address the elephant in the room. If they dealt with what happened six years ago, then maybe the tension between them would dissipate, hopefully taking his desire for her with it. He really needed to stop thinking about Emily Arnott and all the wonderful and wicked things he'd like to do to, and with, her.

"Let's talk about that night," Matt suggested, hitting the button to get the elevator to stop.

The car shuddered to a halt and Emily scowled at him. "Let's not. And restart the elevator, Velez."

Matt wasn't the type to take orders from anyone. "I'm sorry I hurt your feelings but you were drunk and I don't take advantage of drunk young girls."

It was the truth but only a fraction of it.

Emily's eyes contained chips of ice. "You also told me I wasn't your type."

Did he say that? Man, he was an even bigger idiot than he thought.

"And ten minutes after you swatted me away, you had your hand on the ass of another blonde in a black dress."

Matt winced, now remembering. He'd been so tempted to go back and find Emily but, knowing he shouldn't and couldn't, found a very inadequate substitute. And he'd obviously hurt Emily's feelings, and that he did regret.

"I am sorry," Matt said, hoping she'd believe him. "Will you please forgive me and can I take you to dinner to make it up to you?"

Where the hell did that suggestion come from? He was supposed to be staying far away from her!

Shock crossed Emily's face, quickly followed by panic. Closing her eyes, she muttered a quiet but quite dirty curse. Not something he thought he'd hear falling from her lips. Well, well. Interesting to realize that the blonde wasn't as angelic as he thought.

Good to know.

Emily opened her eyes and when she stepped toward him, Matt sucked in a breath…was she making a move on him? All thoughts of distance and moving on evaporated and all Matt could think was that he couldn't wait to taste her, to peel that dress off her slim but curvy body, to kiss the tender skin behind her knee, to dip his tongue into her belly button, to skate his hand over her sexy butt. They'd be good together; he just knew it. Good? Hell, they'd probably set the bed on fire.

Matt lowered his head so that she didn't have to stretch her neck to kiss him; her silver heels gave her another two inches of height but she still only came up to his shoulder. His eyelids started to lower and he held his breath, thinking that he'd waited a long, long time to do this...

But instead of his heart lurching when her mouth met his, the elevator shot upward as she slammed her open hand against the button and Matt was caught off-balance, physically and mentally.

Emily sent him an evil smile and her hand came up to pat his cheek. "Did you really think that I'd just fall into your arms because having me now works for you?"

The doors to the elevator opened and Emily sent him a smile cold enough to freeze the balls off a brass monkey.

"Six years ago, I thought you were my cup of tea, but I drink champagne now."

Matt watched her walk away, thinking she was a beguiling mixture of sexy, sensitive and savage. And, because he was obviously an idiot, she was also now a hundred times more intriguing.

And that, to a man who thought the height of commitment was an occasional sleepover and breakfast the next morning, was terrifying.

Matt felt the vibration on his wrist, looked down at his watch and saw that his phone was sending him multiple alerts. Frowning, he tapped the black screen and stared at the colorful map. It took him a moment, maybe two, to work out that the dot flying down the road leading away from the country club was his car, his brand new, stupidly powerful AMG Roadster and that someone—a certain choirboy-looking valet— was taking it on a joyride.

The little shit. Matt just prayed that the same god of stupidity who'd protected him when he was sixteen was on duty tonight and that the kid didn't find himself wrapped around a light pole.

What else could go wrong, Matt wondered as he stepped out of the elevator.

As it turned out, quite a lot, actually.

She didn't have the time or the inclination to deal with the still-sexy Matt Velez, Emily thought as she stepped out of the elevator and headed for the ballroom, the diamond ring on her left ring finger both heavy and hot.

And why, oh why, did her body still betray her every time she and Matt shared the same air? Her heart started to sprint, her boobs tightened, her nipples ached and yep, the space between her thighs heated. Her eyes kept going to his sensual mouth; she wanted to trace his thick brows with her thumb, run

her fingers over his flat stomach and over the masculine bulge in his pants.

Six years had flown by but her lust for Matt hadn't
diminished. *So* annoying.

Emily glanced down at the unfamiliar ring and
all thoughts of the smoldering and ripped Matteo
Velez retreated as her stomach flew up to lodge in
her esophagus, cutting off her air supply.

Yesterday, her life was normal, maybe even a little
boring. Tonight, she was, very temporarily, engaged
to a raging lunatic.

How the hell had it happened?

Unable to face the crowds within the ballroom,
people she'd known since she was a child, Emily
walked down the hallway and slipped inside a small,
thankfully empty meeting room. Gripping the back
of a chair, she dipped her head and stared down at
the expensive carpet, trying to get her nausea under
control.

She kept to herself, worked hard, obeyed the rules,
tried her best. Why was this happening to her?

Emily heard the door open behind her and she
whirled around, releasing a relieved sigh when she
saw Gina closing the door after her. Gina, her oldest
friend and her PA at Arnott's Wealth Management,
hurried over to her and placed her hands on Emily's
shoulders, her expression radiating her concern.

"I saw you stomping away from Matt Velez. Did
you have words with him? Did he upset you?"

Emily snorted. She wished Matt Velez was the sum
total of her problems. She could handle him with one

hand behind her back. "Like I would allow Falling Brook's part-time lothario to upset me. I've been calling you and I left a bunch of messages."

"Phone died and I had company," Gina replied.

Situation normal. Not knowing where to start, Emily lifted her hand and showed Gina the solitaire diamond ring on her finger. Gina gripped her hand, confused. "What? What the hell is this?"

"I am, apparently, engaged to Nico Morris."

Gina stared at her until a smile hit her eyes. "Okay, that's funny. Like you'd allow that toad to put a ring on your finger."

Oh, how Emily wished it was a joke. And she didn't blame Gina for not believing her, as she'd told Nico on their last date a few weeks ago that they could only be friends, that she wasn't interested in a relationship with him or anyone else. She'd kept her explanation simple, not bothering to explain that she was perfectly content being on her own, that she'd witnessed the devastation love could cause and she wanted no part of it. Emily clearly remembered how emotionally eviscerated she felt when her mom left, withdrawing her love.

Marriage, children…a life intertwined with someone who might leave her swinging in the wind wasn't an option. She wasn't that brave. Or that stupid.

"Nope, it's his ring and this is what I'm doing."

Gina stared at her and when Emily didn't smile, she lifted her hand to her mouth. "Why the hell did you say yes? You told him that you weren't interested in him, didn't you?"

And that, Emily was convinced, was the catalyst for his crazy proposal. Nico wasn't a man who could deal with rejection.

Gina took her finger and tried to pull the ring off. "Take this off and tell him that you had a rush of blood to the brain and that you can't, won't marry him. What the hell is wrong with you, Emily?"

Emily curled her fingers and tugged her hand from Gina's grip.

"He's had affairs with married women, been involved in some dodgy deals and nobody can trust a word he says. He's beyond redemption," Gina muttered. She glared at Emily. "I can understand him wanting to marry you but why the hell would you say yes?"

And here came the sticky part, the part she couldn't, shouldn't, reveal. But she had to tell someone and Gina was her go-to person, the only person she could trust with this information. She couldn't run to her dad—she'd never been able to—and she hadn't had any contact with her mom since she did a runner twelve-plus years ago.

She was, as always, on her own. Well, apart from Gina…

"You can't tell anyone, Gee, not one soul, but… He's blackmailing me."

Gina frowned, obviously puzzled. "What?"

Emily repeated her statement. "Last night he came by, told me that I'm what he wants in a wife and that he loves the idea of being married to Falling Brook's angel—" Emily pulled a disgusted face "—and marrying me will improve his standing in the community."

Gina frowned. "But blackmail implies that he has something on you."

And he did. "Nico went with me to Brook Village once, to meet Davy, and Dad was there. Dad was in the coffee shop, sitting with another parent of a resident, a guy we know by the name of John. He and Dad were deep in discussion and I was thrilled because, as you know, Dad doesn't have friends or interact with people outside the office."

"I don't understand how this relates to you being blackmailed," Gina complained, gesturing for her to hurry up with her explanation.

"John, as Nico told me, is the English name for Ivan. The man Dad was talking to was Ivan Sokolov, the head of the Russian mob up and down the East Coast, from Maine to Miami. Unknown to me, Nico managed to take a series of photographs of him and Dad enjoying a cozy chat."

Gina threw up her hands, confused. "I don't get it."

"Nico wants to marry me and if I don't agree, he's going to start a rumor, backed up by the photographs, that Arnott's Wealth Management is laundering money for the Russian mob. Dad, despite being a workaholic and a social recluse, is incredibly well respected and has built a business on honesty and integrity and the slightest hint of being associated with the mob will destroy our reputation."

Gina's mouth fell open. "You're joking."

Emily shook her head. She wished she was.

"Why is Nico doing this?" Gina cried, tears in her eyes.

Emily looked away, also feeling the burn of a fast-approaching crying jag. But tears wouldn't help; they never had before.

"He told me, quite openly, that he doesn't like being rejected and that he's determined to have me, one way or another. He's also quite fond of the idea of marrying the town princess, someone respectable and who is an integral part of the Falling Brook community."

Emily blew out a long breath. "I'm not, obviously, going to marry him. I'd rather die. I only agreed to wear his ring because I need time to think."

Gina dropped to sit on the edge of the chair. "God, Em, what are you going to do?"

Emily looked down at the ring, scowling. "Play along until I find a way to extricate myself from the situation and save Arnott's without putting our reputation at risk. And I will, have no doubt. I'm not marrying Nico Morris, or anyone else."

Marriage, after all, was just another word for adopting an overgrown man-child with issues. Not for her, thank you very much.

And Morris was an idiot if he thought she'd just nod and acquiesce. She was stronger and tougher than her good-girl reputation and angelic face suggested.

Two

An hour later—after inspecting his undamaged car and tearing a strip off the kid for his unauthorized use of his expensive vehicle—Matt returned to the ballroom and handed his ticket to the bubbly blonde standing at the door to the function room, refusing her offer of a free cocktail. The hostess offered to accompany him into the room and Matt didn't miss the interested gleam in her eye. If he hadn't encountered Emily earlier, he might've considered her offer for some conversation, a couple of drinks and the silent invitation for bed-based fun later.

But, while he wouldn't object to some no-strings-attached sex, she wasn't the woman he wanted to have no-strings sex with. Matt smoothed down his tie, looking around the packed room, and scowled when he couldn't see Emily.

This was classic déjà vu: the same ballroom and the same woman on his mind.

He needed a drink so Matt headed toward the bar, greeting people along the way. He'd grown up in this town—albeit on the wrong side of the tracks—and was a familiar face in Falling Brook. It didn't bother Matt that many of the residents of Falling Brook remembered him for being the town's bad boy, the rebel, the kid with a chip as big as a redwood on his shoulder. It did bother him that whenever he moved in circles such as these, a part of him still felt like he should perform or impress to feel valued.

He'd rather die than admit it but, here in Falling Brook, despite being known as one of the youngest CEOs in a dynamic Manhattan investment firm, he occasionally still felt like that lost kid, eclipsed by his older brother and seldom seen by his parents and teachers.

For a while he'd given up, run wild, but when he went away to college, his innate competitive streak—and not having to compete against a once-in-a-lifetime genius—shot him to the top of his class. Winning became his drug of choice and being anything less than exceptional was unacceptable. He succeeded at nearly everything he tried.

Except for love and relationships.

Matt didn't play that game at all. Love was a tool his family wielded, or in his case, never used at all.

It was better to keep his distance, to operate on

the surface when it came to relationships. It was far easier to exit the shallows than fight the currents in the open ocean.

At the bar, Matt ordered a whiskey and looked around, wondering where Emily Arnott was. Matt pulled a face; the room was filled with gorgeous women but he couldn't get his mind off Emily.

She was like a particularly annoying, sexy-assin itch he couldn't get rid of. Maybe if he stopped avoiding her and made an active effort to get her into bed—for a night or for a weekend—he could stop fantasizing about her. He was an experienced guy and he knew that the reality was never as good as his imagination but, in Emily Arnott's case, he needed to test the theory to believe it.

But, judging by her cold and snarky attitude earlier, he had a snowball's chance in hell of that happening.

Shit.

"Matt."

Matt turned slowly, instantly recognizing the voice of Joshua Lowell. He'd thrown his hat in the ring as a replacement for Joshua Lowell's job, the CEO position at Black Crescent. After a few meetings with Joshua, he was waiting on his decision. An offer, so he'd heard, had been made to another top contender, but the guy had turned it down—all good news for Matt. He wasn't sure he would take the job but Matt liked to keep his options open.

"Joshua." Matt shook Joshua's hand and gestured to the bar. "Can I buy you a drink?"

Joshua nodded, ordered a whiskey and tapped a long finger on the surface of the bar. "How's it going?"

Matt shrugged. "Always good."

Matt noticed Nico Morris approaching the bar and deliberately turned his back on his one-time, incredibly annoying colleague. Ignoring Morris, which was not difficult, Matt turned his attention back to Joshua. They exchanged casual conversation about mutual acquaintances and Matt knew that Joshua was waiting for him to ask whether he'd come to a decision about the CEO position at Black Crescent. Matt never did what was expected so he just handed Joshua a cool smile.

"I'm still debating who would be best to take over from me and I hope to make a final decision soon," Joshua eventually answered Matt's unasked question.

"I gathered. But we both know that I'm the best qualified, have great instincts and have the track record to prove it." It wasn't a boast; he could fully back up any claims he made.

"Yeah, I'm fully aware that MJR Investing's profits have tripled since you became CEO."

"That's my job." One he was damn good at. Matt smiled. "I'd hire me if I was you."

One of the reasons he'd been hoping for an offer from Black Crescent was because he was about to renegotiate his contract with MJR Investing. An offer from a rival firm would make his board of directors that much more amenable to his demands of a significant salary increase, more company stock and, most important, more autonomy.

Matt decided it was a good time to change the subject. "Congratulations on your engagement."

Joshua's smile reached the eyes that immediately went to Sophie, his fiancée, standing across the room. "Thanks. We're happy."

"Have you started painting again?" Matt asked, genuinely interested.

Joshua grimaced. "I'm so out of practice."

Joshua excused himself to find his fiancée, taking another whiskey and Sophie's champagne with him. Matt was about to start working the room when a hard hand gripped his shoulder. He spun around and relaxed when Zane Patterson stepped into the space Joshua Lowell had vacated.

Matt and Zane could trace their friendship back to high school, to when they'd both attended the regional high school instead of the exclusive Falling Brook Prep.

"Still no news on the CEO offer?" Zane asked after ordering a drink from the very busy barman.

Matt shook his head, frustrated. "I'm in a holding position. I can't push for more from MJR until I have a solid offer from Black Crescent. Damn, it's frustrating."

"Yeah, patience was never your thing," Zane commented, lifting his glass in a silent toast.

Matt pushed back his suit jacket to slide his hands into his suit pockets, thinking that Zane looked happier than he did last month. Like so many other people in Falling Brook, Vernon Lowell's disappearance, along with a hefty chunk of Black Crescent's clients' money, deeply affected Zane. Although it had been fifteen years since the Black Crescent Hedge Fund collapsed, its effects still reverberated throughout the community. Matt knew that Sophie's fifteenth-anniversary article painting Josh Lowell as a superhero for rebuilding Black Crescent made Zane fume. He'd freely offered his own insights and photographs to the reporter. He'd also passed along a bombshell DNA test showing Joshua Lowell to be the father of a little girl—but that never made the article. But it didn't matter since the news had already hit the Falling Brook rumor mill.

Matt, because he wasn't the type to beat around the bush, looked Zane in the eye. "The town is speculating wildly, saying you know who sent you the DNA test but you're just being coy."

Zane sighed and shrugged. "I genuinely have no idea who sent it to me. I know *why* they did it—my hatred for the Lowells isn't exactly a secret. The person with the report knew I could be counted on to pass it along."

Matt heard the regret in Zane's voice and a touch of embarrassment. He knew Zane, happy at last and in a relationship with his best friend's sister, would like to put the Lowells and his past behind him. Matt didn't blame him. He preferred not to think of the past either.

Matt always could multitask and he continued to chat to Zane while monitoring the ebb and flow of the room. Nothing seemed out of the ordinary until Matt's eyes flicked over to the door and Zane's voice faded away as Emily Arnott stepped into the room.

And everything else in the room faded… God, she was lovely. And he wanted her more than he needed his heart to beat, his lungs to take in air.

Zane bumped Matt's shoulder with his own, pulling him out of his fantasies of a naked Emily with her legs wrapped around his hips and back into the noisy room. "I cannot believe she is going to marry Nico Morris."

It took a few seconds for his words to make sense, but when they did, Matt wanted to, but couldn't, laugh at Zane's joke. Because he had to be jesting; no way was Emily going to marry that algae-eating pond scum and his ex-colleague, the man who'd made Matt's life hell for two years until Morris left MJR Investing.

"That's not even remotely funny, Patterson."

Zane frowned. "Damn right, it's not. Nico is a sleazeball."

Matt's heart plummeted to his toes. "You're *not* joking?"

"I never joke about Morris," Zane said, his expression grim, gesturing to Emily who now stood next to Morris, his arm around her slim waist.

None of this made sense. Why would someone like Emily marry someone like Nico Morris? Nico was one of the least-popular people in Falling Brook and for good reason. He lied, he cheated and he'd amassed a list of enemies as long as his spine. While Matt collected and acted on information he received, he never used said information as a carrot or a stick. Nico, by comparison, used every dirty trick in the book.

Their animosity went back to when Nico was still employed by MJR Investing, before he left the company to go out on his own. Matt was on the fast track while Nico's prospects for career advancement had hit the ceiling. Nico spread rumors about him and actively tried to sabotage his career.

Morris had been a constant pain in his ass back then but Matt was, mostly, over his childish antics.

But Nico having Emily Arnott, the woman he considered to be the one who got away, was completely unacceptable.

Matt was the one with the glittering career, the fast cars and the fat bank accounts, so why was he even bothering to compete with Morris? Maybe it was because competition was in his blood and he hated feeling like he was a step behind.

But Nico and Emily marrying? Yeah, well, that wasn't going to happen.

Hours later, and after fielding what felt to be a hundred curious, surprised and shocked congratulations on her engagement, Emily walked down the hallway to the bathroom, conscious of a headache building behind her eyes. Nico, thank God, had left the club already and she could, momentarily, relax.

Oh, how she wished she could rewind her life and erase the past twenty-four hours. She wanted to go back to the person she was yesterday, to her relatively simple and uncomplicated life. And how she wished she could erase her dumb decision to go on a couple of dates with Nico Morris.

Nico could, admittedly, be charming but there was no chemistry between them and that was why she called an end to their brief, unexciting dates.

Yet, not two weeks later, she was engaged to the man!

It was time to go home. If she stayed much longer, she might end up screaming at someone. She'd go home, change into her yoga pants and slug down a glass, or three, of wine and bitch to her cat.

And when she stopped feeling sorry for herself, she'd start thinking of a way to boot Nico from her life without jeopardizing her father's and Arnott's Wealth Management's reputations.

Emily squealed as a strong hand gripped her wrist and tugged her into a small closet adjacent to the meeting room she'd visited earlier. She felt her breasts push into a solid, hard chest. Six years and Matt Velez, damn him, was still as gorgeous as ever. Close-cropped dark hair, those masculine features and a sexy, sexy mouth. Broad shouldered, slim hipped, ripped. And damn, he smelled good.

She loved his eyes; they were the color of a luxurious mahogany mink coat she'd once seen but would never wear, deep and dark and mysterious.

Matt reached behind her to shut the door and they were plunged into darkness. She should be feeling uneasy or even a little scared at Matt's high-handed treatment of her and Emily knew she should blast him but…

But, dammit, she just felt turned on and happy to be in his arms, feeling his heat, his hard body a perfect counterpoint to her soft curves.

She still wanted him.

Emily really wanted not to want him…

Matt lifted his hand off her hip and two seconds later weak light flooded the small room from the dull, bare bulb above them. Matt moved deeper into the closet and rested his elbow on a metal shelf behind him, his deep, dark eyes slamming into hers.

She would not, repeat not, give in to temptation and slam her mouth against his. But she really wanted to…

Emily turned away but then Matt took her hand and she swiftly turned to look back at him. Emily held her breath as he brought her hand to his lips, but instead of kissing her fingers as she expected—wished?—he stopped and his eyes took in the flawless, massive diamond.

"How did I miss this earlier?" he demanded, his voice rough with annoyance.

Emily shrugged. "You were too busy trying to make a half-assed apology."

"Hey, I meant what I said. I am sorry for how I acted that night," Matt said, and Emily heard the sincerity in his tone. She saw his eyes returning to her ring finger and noticed the muscle jumping in his jaw. Matt Velez was not happy at her engagement and the knowledge made her heart tingle.

Stupid thing.

He lifted her hand again and turned the diamond to the dim light. "Boring, as I expected."

Say what? While she didn't like her fiancé, she had to admire the ring. It was a perfect example of a stone with all the four *Cs*—carat weight, cut, color, clarity—and Matt Velez could keep his snarky opinions to himself.

"My ring is exceptional," Emily told him, sounding haughty.

"Knowing Morris, the stone is probably a fake or, at best, manufactured in a factory. Even if it's real, and it's not, it shows his distinct lack of creativity," Matt snapped back. "He could've, at the very least, sprung for a deep blue sapphire from Sri Lanka to match your eyes or a pink diamond to match your lips."

"Do you often go around offering unsolicited advice on engagement rings?"

Matt didn't miss a beat. "Only to a woman who once…" he hesitated and Emily held her breath, dreading his next words. They'd covered this ground earlier and he wouldn't go there, she was sure he wouldn't. "…expressed her interest in seeing me naked."

He went there. Bastard!

"You called me a guppy," Emily shot back. His words and supercilious tone still rankled.

"You were too damn innocent for the grown-up game you were playing," Matt retorted.

Being called innocent because of the way her features were arranged was the bane of her life. And if people didn't think she was innocent then they thought she was stupid or, more often, a combination of the two.

Few bothered to find out if any of their assumptions were true. People tended to get stuck on her face and couldn't imagine her having a conversation about the humanitarian crisis in Darfur or the state of the economy. People, she'd decided, rather liked the idea of her being a bit dim; it was as if they couldn't comprehend Emily being both beautiful and smart.

Her beauty was just a lucky combination of DNA; it didn't mean anything. All it meant was that she'd just won the genetic lottery.

Emily narrowed her eyes at him. "Why did you yank me into this room, Velez? And why are we in a closet when there's a perfectly good meeting room next door?"

"That small room is like Grand Central Station tonight and I don't want to be interrupted," Matt retorted. "So, are the rumors true?"

"What rumors?"

"Cut the crap, Emily," Matt snapped. "Tell me that you aren't engaged to Morris?" His thumb tapped the stone, his fingers still holding her captured hand.

God, she wished she could. "I am. And why are you suddenly so interested in my life?"

Before Matt could answer, a deep voice drifted through the thin walls of the closet. "Why are we meeting in this room instead of at the bar?"

Emily's eyes widened at the strange voice and Matt

tipped his head. He dropped his mouth to speak in her ear. "That's Joshua Lowell speaking."

Emily nodded.

"I got a birthday gift in the mail yesterday."

"Oliver." Matt mimed the word. "His brother, I think."

"Bit late, isn't it? Your birthday was last month," Joshua commented.

Emily reached up to speak in Matt's ear. "We should go."

Matt's hand rested on her hip and she felt the heat of his fingers through the thin fabric of her dress. Sparks skidded up her spine and her mouth felt dry. "If we do, they'll know we're in here and it might get back to Morris. Better to wait until the room and hallway are clear. I'd hate to be the one to cause friction between you and your fiancé."

Emily narrowed her eyes at him, hearing the sarcasm in his voice. She had no doubt Matt Velez didn't give a fig for Nico's, or anybody else's, opinion.

"The gift was a fishing pole, accompanied by an ultrabrief message. One word. 'Someday.'"

Matt shrugged when Emily lifted her eyebrows. Obviously, he was equally unsure of why Oliver was making a big deal about receiving a fishing pole and a cryptic note.

"Do you remember when Dad used to take you fishing?" Oliver asked.

"Wow, that's a memory from way back when. And yes, I remember—it's not like it happened that often," Joshua replied.

"Dad promised to take me fishing not too long before he disappeared," Oliver said, sounding hesitant. "Josh…do you think…"

"That it could be from Dad? That he's trying to let you know he's alive?" Joshua rushed his sentence and Emily felt Matt tense beside her. He mimed the word wow and Emily felt guilty for listening in on a private conversation.

"No, Oliver. I don't think it's that. I think it's someone trying to mess with your head. And if I find out who it is, I'm going to rip his head off his shoulders."

"I've been clean for a long time, Joshua. And I'm not a fragile piece of china."

Matt raised his eyebrows. "Issues?"

"Cocaine," Emily whispered.

How nice that Oliver had a big brother, someone he could rely on, Emily thought. Since the time she was fourteen, she became the "mom" of the house, shopping, cooking and trying to connect with her distant and workaholic dad.

She put on a smile, did everything right at home, pretending that she wasn't gutted that the person who was supposed to love her the most had left her to deal with a distant father and a brother with special needs. She adored Davy but she'd been so young to assume adult responsibilities and her mom, by leaving, stole her childhood, her teenage years and her confidence.

"I feel stupid," Oliver said from the other side of the wood paneling, pulling Emily's reluctant attention back to the conversation on the other side of the thin wall.

"Don't," Joshua replied. "Listen, the Lowells are always going to be targeted, thanks to what Dad did and the mess he left behind. You're not the only one who's been trolled, Ol."

Joshua hesitated before continuing and Emily had to admit that Matt was right, this was riveting stuff. It was wrong to eavesdrop but, like anything to do with the Lowells, this was a fascinating discussion.

"Sophie came to me and told me that she had a DNA report showing me to be the father of a baby girl born four years ago. I was, naturally, stunned," Joshua explained.

"You have a baby girl?"

"No, you idiot, I don't. I was always careful and none of my previous partners even hinted at me getting them pregnant. But the report looked totally authentic so Soph and I looked into it. We found out that the report was generated by a doctor with a long and torrid history of shady practices and false results. When I heard that, I was relieved—with our family history, I didn't want to be a dad."

"I hear you on that," Oliver fervently agreed. "We didn't exactly have a great role model to emulate—we'd be terrible fathers. Well, I know I would. I don't want kids."

Joshua's voice held the hint of a smile. "I was convinced I didn't either but I think I might, want a child, that is. I figure that Sophie will keep our kid on the straight and narrow and I'll take my cues from her."

"You are a braver man than I am, big brother. It's

hard enough to look after myself—I don't want or need the responsibility of parenthood."

Emily heard the click of high heels and the door to the meeting room opened. "Guys, the auction is in the ballroom. Why are you in here?"

Was that Sophie's voice? Emily heard the shuffle of big feet as the Lowell brothers left the room. When silence fell, Emily reached for the door handle and eased the door open. She peeked outside and saw that the hallway was empty. Time for her to go.

It would take all her willpower to walk away from Matt when all she really wanted was to step into his arms, feed off his strength, taste his mouth. Strip his clothes...

Right, enough of that, Arnott.

"You take girls to all the best places, Velez," Emily said, making sure her voice was just a degree warmer than frozen nitrogen.

Matt tipped his head to the side and jammed his hands into the pockets of his suit pants. "Don't marry him, Emily. You'll regret it."

She started to tell him that she'd regret marriage, period, but just kept herself from uttering the words. Emily sucked in a calming breath and, looking him in the eye, raised her stubborn chin. "I'm sure your opinion matters...to someone."

Matt had the temerity to smile. "I'm going to change your mind, princess. Someday my opinion is the only one you're going to care about."

Emily lifted her hand to her brow, pretending to

scan the environment. "And there goes a flying pig dressed in a pink tutu."

Emily picked up the skirt of her floor-skimming dress and stepped into the empty hall. "Goodbye, Matteo."

"This isn't over." Matt's words, spoken in his deep voice, rumbled over her skin.

Oh God, she really hoped it was because she didn't know if she could cope with both Nico and Matt.

Damn, but she needed a stiff drink. At home, while she was cuddling her cat. She was, officially, peopled out.

Three

The next evening, Matt rapped on the door to Emily's above-garage apartment, wondering what the hell he was doing on her doorstep on a Sunday at twilight. But since leaving the auction the previous night, he couldn't purge the image of Emily's head on Morris's shoulder, her hand tucked into his arm, his damned ring on her finger.

Was he simply envious Morris had a woman he wanted? So envious that he was prepared to, for the first time in his life, chase after a woman when his normal modus operandi was to let women chase him?

He'd lain awake for most of the night, thinking of the past and the present.

He'd been so young when he encountered Emily and yes, she'd knocked him off his feet. But he was older now and he could easily dismiss his initial thoughts of her being part of his forever as wishful, fanciful thinking. He didn't believe in love and forever.

The only reason he was here was because he wanted her...

Wanted her enough for him to make more of an effort than he normally did. He also wasn't the type who made a move on another man's woman but Morris was a dick, and honor, after all the crap Morris pulled years ago, didn't count in this situation.

And sure, he was a competitive SOB and, at the best of times—i.e. anything that didn't involve Emily Arnott—he didn't like someone else having something or someone he wanted. And he did want Emily, he'd wanted her six years ago and he wanted her now, and the thought of taking her away from Morris warmed his cold heart.

He would also be doing her a huge favor because he knew just how much of a dick Morris could be.

The snap of fingers in front of his face brought Matt back to the present and he focused on intense purple-blue eyes fringed with thick, dark lashes. Emily's straight blond hair was raked back from her forehead into a high ponytail and her face was free of makeup. She wore a baggy sweatshirt, leggings and fuzzy socks, and every inch of him craved her.

A massive black, brown and gray cat meowed, sat on her foot and lifted its enormous head, eyes on the sandwich in her hand.

Speaking of which, Matt hadn't eaten all day. He

lifted the top slice of bread and frowned. "Cheese? And…" He wrinkled his nose. "Is that pineapple?"

"And jalapeño chilies and salt and pepper."

Ugh. That sounded gross. "Are you pregnant?"

He looked down at her flat stomach. Was that why she was marrying jerk-face; to give her child a father? When did women start having pregnancy cravings?

"No, I'm not pregnant," Emily replied, annoyed. "I just happen to like weird combinations of food. Chicken-liver paté and marmalade, pickles and Oreos."

Yuck. "So, you'll know you're pregnant when you start craving peanut butter and jelly, cheese and ham?" Matt asked.

A hint of humor momentarily penetrated the frost in her eyes. "Why are you here, Velez?"

Matt waited for her to invite him in but when she didn't budge, he sighed. "Let me in, Emily. We need to talk."

Emily rolled her eyes, obviously exasperated, but she gestured him inside. Matt stepped over the massive furball and placed his hands into the pockets of his pants, taking in her apartment. He immediately felt at home, thinking he could kick off his shoes and sink down into that comfortable sofa. The apartment was spacious, with wide wooden windows looking out to the forest behind her dad's house, and beyond that to the mountains. The apartment itself was a mishmash of colors and styles, in blues and greens with hints of pink, but nothing jarred.

Black-and-white prints of exotic places—he recognized the Imperial Citadel at Hanoi and Syntagma Square in Athens—covered her walls. He stepped up to them, captured by the moody atmosphere and the way the photographer played with the shadows. "These are brilliant. Who took them?"

"I did. I traveled solo for a few months after leaving college."

The cat did a figure eight between his legs and Matt bent down to scratch him between his ears. "What's his name?"

"Fatty."

Matt smiled. "Unoriginal but appropriate."

Emily placed her sandwich on the plate on the island counter, leaned her forearms on the counter and pinned him to the floor with her direct gaze. "What do you want?"

You. Naked. As soon as possible.

Too much? Too strong? Yeah, obviously.

Matt ran his hand through his hair as he turned to face her. "Why are you wearing that ridiculously big ring? Why are you really marrying Morris? And don't tell me it's because you love him."

"Maybe I do."

"BS."

When he got out of his head, pushed aside his envy and jealousy—and his need to have her—and applied logic to the situation he still, instinctively, had the feeling their engagement was a sham. He'd watched her last night and nothing in the way she acted told him that she was in love or was even excited about her engagement. She accepted good wishes and congratulations with a pained smile and her responses had been too deliberate, too thought out.

Too choreographed.

Living on the outside of his family, not being a part of that inner circle of three, had honed his observation and perception skills. He could read body language as well as he could walk and talk and something about Emily and her response to being newly engaged was off.

"Are you in trouble?" he demanded, his voice rough.

Emily's big round eyes widened in a too-practiced-to-be-real move. It instantly made her look younger and upped her innocence factor. But underneath the forced insouciance was panic and he wanted to know why.

"No, I'm not in trouble. And even if I was, why would I confide in you?" Emily asked, tipping her head to the side. "We're barely acquaintances. I'm just another girl who threw herself at you, one of the few you didn't bother to catch."

She was pissed because he didn't take her up on her drunk offer? Well, he was pissed off too. He would never tell her his reaction to her scared the crap out of him and that he'd been so tempted to throw caution to the wind and start something meaningful with her...

Thank God he hadn't. Attraction faded and love never lasted.

"You were a kid and you'd been drinking," Matt said, pushing his words through gritted teeth, using that same, probably tired, excuse. "Tipsy or not, I don't take advantage of young girls."

Her next question shocked the hell out of him. "And if I asked you that same question last night?"

He didn't hesitate. "You'd still be naked, in my bed." He gestured to the short hallway. "Or naked, in your bed. My place or here, trust me, you still wouldn't be wearing a stitch of clothing."

Matt watched as color flooded her face, entranced as her eyes darkened to a color similar to those African violets his mother had nurtured on the windowsill of their kitchen. Within those dark depths he saw passion, desire, the fight for control of both. Her eyes dropped to his mouth and Matt knew she wanted what he did—their lips fused, a taste of each other's breath.

He moved, or did she, and then her fingers were on the back of his neck and his hands were on her hips and he bent down and she rose up and then...

God. *Perfection.*

Soft lips with a hint of pineapple, a flowery scent in his nose and a soft, surprisingly curvy body in his arms. Needing more, needing everything, Matt pulled her closer and Emily released a tiny sound when her breasts pushed into his chest and moaned again when his tongue swept into her mouth.

Emily seemed to sag against him and Matt wrapped his arms around her slim back, lifting her up and into him, happily taking her weight. Her fingers came to rest on his jawline, as soft and arousing as a feather.

Matt felt Emily's foot run up the back of his calf,

felt her hands on his back, on his butt. She, thank God, wanted him back. This time, he wouldn't hesitate; this time, he'd do everything to her that he couldn't do all those years ago.

He'd start by kissing her from tip to toe...

Matt pulled his mouth off hers and started the exploration of her face, nibbling the fine line of her jaw, tasting the skin on those cut-glass cheekbones. Her nose was straight and just a little haughty...

It took a minute, maybe more for him to realize that Emily was a stiff board in his arms, that her hands were on his chest, trying to push him, not very emphatically, away. Matt groaned, blinked and tried to get his eyes to focus on her face.

If she wanted to stop, he might just drop to the floor and howl.

"Velez! Stop!"

Yep, crap, she wanted to stop. Matt cursed silently and allowed her to slide down his body, swallowing his moan of frustration. He lifted his hands off her and stepped away. It nearly killed him but that's what grown men did. He might not have any honor when it came to poaching on Morris's territory but when a woman said no, he listened.

Emily made a fist, put it to her mouth and Matt caught the terror in her eyes, the waves of blue-and-purple panic.

"What the hell am I doing?" Emily whispered and, while her words were low, he caught her fear. "This is madness."

Matt's protective instincts kicked in and he took a

step toward her, cursing when she scuttled backward, her hands up to ward him off.

"Em, Jesus, what is going on with you?"

"Nothing, I keep telling you that!" Emily said, pointing to her front door. "I just need you to leave. Now. Immediately."

Matt thought about arguing but Em had not only physically retreated, she'd pulled back mentally, as well. There was nothing he could say or do to recapture the magic of their kiss, to put her back in his arms.

Matt jammed his hands into the pockets of his chinos, hoping his expression didn't reveal his frustration. Emily Arnott was less of a pushover and more stubborn—and more loyal, a quality Morris did not deserve!—than he expected.

He rather liked that.

But, under his envy and his lust, his gut instinct was screaming that there was something fishy about their engagement and he was the only one who realized it. He'd allow her to think that he was minding his own business, walking away, but he'd be back.

Sometimes, the only way to gain ground was to retreat.

The next morning, in her corner office at Arnott's Wealth Management, Emily stared at her computer screen, the numbers and letters blurring in front of her eyes. As the company's operations manager, she needed to stay sharp, but she was operating on less than three hours of sleep. She'd also spent the bulk of last night staring at her ceiling, her thoughts bouncing between how to save herself from becoming a trophy wife and how good she felt standing in Matt's arms, how wonderful it was to be kissed by him.

Why she was thinking about Matt Velez when her entire life was falling apart at the seams, God only knew.

Emily dropped her forehead to her sleek desk and banged her head against the smooth surface. So Matt kissed her, big deal. Or it would've been, two weeks or so ago. But really, since she was being blackmailed into marriage, she shouldn't be thinking about his dark eyes or his soft lips, the muscled body under those designer suits and his sexy scent.

Velez wasn't important; saving Arnott's reputation and, obviously, getting out of her engagement was.

Emily sat up and spun her chair around to face the window behind her. While it was still, technically, summer, there was a slight chill in the air and hints of fall in the changing color of the trees. Fall was her favorite season and she usually took a week's vacation after Labor Day. This year she'd planned to fly down to Grand Cayman to spend a week in a friend's cottage overlooking a private beach. She'd planned to lie in the sun, read a dozen books, catch fish and cook them over an open fire. Drink wine.

Chill.

Well, those plans had been blown out of the water.

She couldn't go anywhere, do anything until she dis-engaged herself and protected the company bearing her name.

Telling anybody, other than Gina, about Nico's blackmail scheme was out of the question. She couldn't even take the problem to her dad. Oh, she'd told him she was engaged, but Leonard had barely reacted—had he actually not heard her or did he simply not care? Davy wouldn't understand the implications of her actions and, as for her mom, well, she'd rather walk through a field of Christ's-thorn than tell her mom anything...

And, Lord, what was Nico thinking? This wasn't the eighteen hundreds when a man's standing was improved by marriage; these days you lived and died by your own choices. Sure, she came from a good family, and the Arnotts were one of the first families to settle in Falling Brook. And yeah, back when her dad liked people and before her mom left, Leonard was the unofficial mayor of the town, her mom one of its most popular hostesses.

But those halcyon days were gone, her dad was wrapped up in business and the little time he spent outside of work was spent either with Davy or in his home gym.

Her mom wasn't the only one who'd abandoned her. Her mom physically disappeared but while her dad was physically present—working in his office down the hallway—he was as mentally absent as her mother.

She'd finally learned to be independent and self-sufficient, to rely on herself and to trust her decisions. But Em sometimes wished she had someone to rely on, someone who she could talk to and who understood the issues around her father's emotional distance and her brother's special needs.

While she loved her independence, occasionally she got really tired of being a tribe of one. But being lonely was still better than being constantly disappointed by people for wanting and expecting more than they could give her. Still, she craved a strong father and a mother who could remember her name.

Love…why did people constantly look for it?

She'd veered off her original thought…why was Nico so determined to have her that he'd resorted to blackmail? And, admittedly, his threat was a good one. They had some run-of-the-mill clients but they also worked in a niche market—looking after the financial needs of vulnerable adults—and Arnott's reputation meant everything to them. One whiff of scandal would have their clients running for the hills.

Nico told her that their marriage would bring him more clients, better opportunities, but Emily knew he was overestimating her importance in the small, wealthy community of Falling Brook.

And, while she desperately wanted to, she didn't believe him when he said that he wasn't in a rush to sleep with her. He touched her too frequently—a stroke down her arm, a hand low on her back, almost touching her butt—and she saw the desire in his eyes.

He was smart enough not to push her, to scare her more than she already was, but Em knew he wanted her—in his bed, as his wife, to make him look better by marrying into one of the "famous" families of Falling Brook—and he was desperate enough to blackmail her.

Emily abruptly stood up, frustrated. She had to figure out how to paralyze Nico, without endangering the company. Gina was looking for gossip, reaching out to her contacts for anything she could use but so far, she'd come up with nothing.

There had to be more she could do. Thanks to her big blue eyes and long blond hair and the stereotype associated with women who looked like her, few people realized Emily had a sharp brain behind her pretty face. What she really needed to do was to push Nico into a corner, to shut down his options. She needed information on Nico of greater or equal importance to what he had on her. It was imperative that she put him in a similar situation as he'd shoved her into, one where he was equally at risk.

But that meant pretending to be his fiancée while digging up damaging information on him. Emily leaned her shoulder into the window, scowling down at the busy road below her. Her only advantage was that Nico thought she was a little dim and naive and docile.

She wasn't. And she wasn't the type to go down without a damn good fight.

In his office in Midtown Manhattan, Matt threw his pen onto the desk and gripped the bridge of his nose between his thumb and forefinger, wishing he could squeeze a certain blonde out of his head.

He'd been up since four, checking the Asian markets, moving millions around with the touch of his mouse, the tap of his keyboard. As CEO, he wasn't expected to work the markets but he liked to keep his hand in so he still managed the portfolios of a handful of carefully selected clients. In six hours, he'd traded more than fifty million USD, making a small profit on both his own and his clients' money. On good days, trading was the best job in the world and a massive profit in one session could keep a smile on his face for hours. It could also be, on bad days, the equivalent of riding through hell, naked, sitting on the shell of a superslow snail. On days that trades went against him, resulting in a significant loss, he frequently prayed for his heart to stop so he didn't have to hear the blood rushing through his system, the taste of bile in the back of his throat, the cramping of his stomach.

This morning was a so-so day, minor profits, acceptable losses, resulting in a net profit of a couple of percent. Not his best day but also not his worst. Considering that thoughts of a violet-eyed blonde kept strolling through his brain, he'd done okay.

Luckily.

Reaching behind him, Matt snagged a bottle of water out of the bar fridge concealed behind a cupboard door and eyed his computer, thinking that he needed to review some reports and make a start on the next quarter's growth projections. Trading was fun but he needed to get down to the real work of managing MJR and, most days, he loved it.

And he would, in a minute. Matt leaned back in his

chair, cracked the top to his water bottle and silently cursed when his mind went back to Emily. What was she up to today?

Before he could wander too far down that unproductive path, Matt heard the rap of knuckles on the frame of his office door and looked up when his senior trader, who also happened to be one of his best friends, strolled through the open door to his office.

Malcolm plopped himself down in the chair opposite Matt and linked his fingers on his flat stomach. "Good day?"

Matt rocked his hand from side to side. "Okayish. You?"

"Some losses this morning. I'm about to dive in again in twenty minutes," Mal replied.

Matt tossed Malcolm a bottle of water before lifting his own bottle to his lips. The reports could wait. "I think I'm going to take the rest of the day off."

Malcolm raised his eyebrows at Matt's statement. Matt couldn't blame him. He was well-known for working longer hours than everyone at the company and was always the first to arrive and the last to leave. "Problem?"

Only a blonde I can't dismiss from my head. Irritation prickled and burned. He was always super focused and it annoyed him that Emily Arnott hovered on the edge of his thoughts for most of the morning.

Two main thoughts kept running through his mind: how good she felt in his arms and how wrong her engagement to Nico Morris was. If she was any other woman, he would've had her in his bed and out of his mind by now.

And she would've left with a smile on her face and a *please call me soon*.

And yes, maybe that did make him sound like a player, but he never made promises he had no intention of keeping. His lovers knew the score…

But Emily kept tipping his world upside down. He wanted to dismiss her, to walk away from this stupid situation, but his mind—or his ego or his pride, or all three bastards working in tandem—just wouldn't let her go. He couldn't walk, not just yet, not until he knew what it was like to make love to her.

Her hold on him pissed him off.

Matt's PA sailed into his office, looking as imperious as a Russian queen. Vee was Matt's right-hand person, someone he trusted more than most. She was also deadly efficient, irascible, abrupt and had few social skills.

Vee had a computer science degree, was a dedicated gamer and occasional hacker, and Matt had no idea why, with her skills, she worked as his PA and office manager.

Vee looked at Malcolm over the top rim of her glasses. "Don't you have work to do, Mr. King?"

Oh, and she also thought that she ran MJR Investing.

Malcolm, not in the least bit intimated, sent her a lazy grin. "Not right now, Miss Vee."

Vee turned her sharp gaze on Matt. "I see you are also slacking off, Mr. Velez."

Vee, despite only being in her late thirties, had the disposition of a Victorian butler and the work ethic, and personality, of a fire ant. Matt adored her.

"I've been at it since four this morning, Vee. Cut me some slack," Matt replied.

Vee sniffed her disapproval. "Never. If I do, this place will fall apart."

Matt rolled his eyes at Malcolm, an action that was rewarded by a dirty look and a purse of ruby-red lips.

"Your messages." Vee slapped a pile of carefully printed slips on his desk. A heavy file landed next to his computer. "Turnover and expense reports."

Malcolm rose, shot him an amused grin and ambled to the door. As he passed through it, Vee ordered him to close it, which he did. Matt, wondering why his PA was being extra bossy, leaned back in his chair and waited for her to speak. Vee was never shy about saying what was on her mind.

"I heard you are talking to Joshua Lowell at Black Crescent."

Matt winced. His potential career move was supposed to be highly confidential but Vee had even better sources in Falling Brook than he did, was far too interested in his life and frequently knew what he was going to eat for dinner before he did. He'd tried to tell her that his personal life was just that, personal, but Vee had just ignored him and deep-dived into his life. A part of Matt rather liked how much she cared; God knew his parents didn't. Never had.

Juan got all of that attention…

"I have no plans to go anywhere, Vee, not yet anyway. I'm just using a potential move to Black Crescent as a bargaining chip with the board." Matt lifted one shoulder. "Unless Black Crescent makes me an offer I simply can't refuse."

"Wherever you go, I go," Vee stated, her tone brooking no argument.

That was a given. Vee was his right hand. And his left. "Maybe," he said, just to tease her.

Vee's bottom lip wobbled, just for a second, and Matt felt guilty. "I'm joking, Vee, of course I'd take you with me," he said, hurrying to reassure her. Vee was a cactus, prickly as hell on the outside with a squishy, easily hurt center.

Vee blinked and dipped her head in a sharp nod. "That's settled then."

"Don't give me grief but I was thinking about taking the rest of the day off," Matt said, pushing his chair back and standing up. "I have a birthday present to buy."

Vee's birthday was next week and he saw the pleasure flash in her eyes. He'd already approved her birthday bonus but he wanted to buy her something special, something that wasn't company related. Vee loved orchids, so he'd ordered a new variety via Falling Brook's nursery and had received word that it had arrived. But Vee would have to receive her birthday present early because houseplants came to him to die.

Vee placed her hand on her heart and sent him a sweet smile. It wasn't one he saw on her face very often, reminding Matt that she needed him as much as he needed her. "Have a good day, Matteo. Is there anything else you need me to do for you?"

Matt rubbed the back of his neck as Emily's gorgeous face drifted through his mind. Maybe Vee knew something he didn't about the Morris/Arnott engagement. But if he asked, his supersharp assistant would immediately sense he was thinking about a woman.

"Do we have any business ties to Arnott's in Falling Brook?" Matt asked, wondering why the thought hadn't occurred to him before. A link between Arnott's and MJR could be exploited to get closer to Emily and what he really wanted, which was her, naked, under him.

Vee, used to his rapid changes of subject, thought for a minute. "Not that I can think of. Of course, every year Emily Arnott asks everyone and anyone who's even vaguely connected to Falling Brook for donations to Brook Village. She also asks for volunteers to join her fundraising committee for the same organization, whatever it may be."

"It's the residential home where her brother lives," Matt explained.

"From the tone of her letter, I thought it was the standard request for time and money. As far as I know, although a few of our clients come from Falling Brook, nobody from MJR has ever volunteered to sit on her committee," Vee added.

Sitting on committees wasn't something he did, but he couldn't keep rocking up unannounced on Emily's doorstep, and if joining her cause got him what he wanted—Emily—he'd suck it up. He needed an excuse to put himself in her orbit. And this was as good a one as any. "When did that request to sit on the fundraising committee come in?"

Vee sent him a what-are-you-up-to look. "Within the last few weeks. If I remember correctly, the first committee meeting is happening this evening, in the boardroom at Arnott's."

"Time?"

"Six p.m." Vee folded her arms across her chest and pursed her lips. "What's going on, Matteo?"

Matt grinned. "A little volunteering is good for the soul, Vee."

"And I'd agree if that was your primary motive," Vee replied, not buying his explanation and not, in any way, impressed with his show of altruism. "Just remember the old saying, Matt…no good deed goes unpunished."

Four

Matt deliberately waited until the fundraising meeting was in progress before sliding into one of the many spare seats at the boardroom table. Emily, quickly covering her shock at his presence, paused in her opening statement to ask him, ever so politely, whether he was lost.

His statement that he wanted to help, in any way he could, was greeted with a small round of applause from the ten other volunteers, all women, but he knew Emily wasn't buying his particular line of BS.

Smart girl.

Forty-five minutes later, Emily called the meeting to a close and thanked her volunteers. Then her eyes clashed with his and he read her order to "sit and stay" as clearly as he read the boring agenda on the table in front of him. Though, he had to admit, Emily plowed through the points of discussion with the ruthless efficiency of a field marshal intent on a quick victory. It was clear that a) she was organized, b) she didn't like to waste time and c) she was passionate about making Brook Village an even better environment for its residents.

Emily Arnott had a sharp brain behind that gorgeous face and Matt was beginning to believe that most people, including him, underestimated her intelligence. And drive.

It was a mistake he wouldn't make again.

Matt stood up as a sleek brunette approached him and took the hand she held out. She introduced herself as Gina, Emily's PA and best friend, and spent a few minutes discussing Brook Village and thanking him for joining Emily's committee.

Behind her as-dark-as-his eyes, he caught her shrewdness and saw her cynicism. He knew she wanted to ask some hard questions, the obvious being *why are you hanging around Emily when you know she's engaged?*

What could he tell her?

That the thought of Nico being engaged to Emily made him sick to his stomach? Sure. He was envious and jealous of her fiancé? Absolutely.

That he wanted Emily more than he wanted to breathe? Triple check.

That he felt out of his depth because women flocked to him and he never overexerted himself in his pursuit of female companionship and this was a strange and unusual situation? God, yes.

"Good night, Gina," Emily stated, her volume button rising.

Gina pointed a finger at Emily and wagged it. "Play nice. We don't have that many volunteers and we can't afford to lose those we do." Gina grinned and Matt noticed the power of her smile. "And he's very nice to look at."

Gina gathered up her bag and her own set of papers and walked out of the room, sending Matt another appreciative glance over her shoulder. He winked at her; she winked back and, with an extra swing of her hips, walked away.

Matt turned his eyes back to Emily and caught her massive eye roll. "You just can't help it, can you?"

"Help what?"

"Flirting. Whether they are old or young, it's like you are hardwired to charm."

Talking to women had never been an issue for him: he liked the species; they liked him back. Up until now, it was a win-win situation.

"She flirted first," Matt replied, keeping his tone mild.

"You are two peas in a pod," Emily muttered.

Matt rested his right buttock on the sturdy table and folded his arms across his chest. "Gina told you that you have to be nice to me," he teased, enjoying the sparks of irritation in her eyes.

"Since Gina works for me and not the other way around, I don't have to listen to her."

"I sympathize—I have a bossy PA, as well."

Emily rubbed her forehead with her fingers and Matt noticed the dark stripes under her eyes. She was exhausted and he couldn't blame her. Being engaged to Morris was enough to keep anyone awake at night.

"I seem to be asking this question a lot but...why are you here?"

Matt thought about spinning a line but decided she could handle the truth. "I want you—I've wanted you every time I've seen you. I'm shocked and confused as to why you're engaged to Morris and I'm not buying your sudden engagement. I don't believe you want to spend the rest of your life with Morris and nothing about this makes sense."

Nothing about his need for her made sense either but Matt decided to keep that to himself.

Surprise jumped in and out of her eyes before her expression turned implacable. Matt found that interesting; if he was wrong, he would've expected anger, some sort of denial of his words.

"I don't care what you think, Velez."

"Oh, I think you do. And I'm also quite curious as to why you kissed me, climbed all over me if you are so in love with your fiancé."

Emily flushed and Matt wondered if she'd blush like that if she was naked and he was admiring her beautiful body. He hauled in a deep breath, conscious that the fabric covering his groin was a fraction tighter. He'd never wanted anyone more...

And would he want her so much if she wasn't off-limits?

Man, he couldn't remember when last, if ever, he gave a woman this much headspace.

Emily opened her mouth to blast him but the words died on her lips. Instead of laying into him, she dropped into her chair and rested her forearms on her knees and stared at the floor. Matt, his attraction to her instantly forgotten as he'd caught the flash of panic in her eyes before she looked down, moved over to her and dropped to balance on his toes, his own arm on his bent knee. "Em, talk to me. Help me understand."

Emily continued to stare at the carpet and Matt kept his eyes on her face. Up close, he noticed how thick her lashes were, that she had a spray of freckles under her carefully applied makeup and that she had a tiny hole in the side of her nose. Emily had once worn a nose stud or ring and the thought intrigued him. Did a free spirit live under her Goody-Two-shoes, do-no-wrong, conservative persona?

Emily opened her mouth to speak, shook her head and slammed her lips closed. She pushed back her chair and rose to her feet.

Matt looked up at her and slowly stood. Ignoring him, she placed her papers into a fabric folder and closed the lid to her laptop.

He waited for her to face him again, knowing the moment had passed and that she wasn't going to open up. When she turned to acknowledge him, her remote expression confirmed that she'd shored up her defense. "Why are you hassling me? Is this what you do? Do you get off on pursuing women who are in committed relationships?"

The derision in her voice sliced through him and he fought the urge to hurl a couple of insults back. She was the only one who'd ever tempted him to engage and that was so out of character. Matt kept his emotional distance; if a woman refused his advances, he shrugged her off and moved on.

But Emily Arnott had crawled under his skin and stayed there. Part of it was flat-out desire; part of it was envy that Nico had something that Matt wanted—

Envy, one of the seven deadly sins. Matt was competitive and Nico was one of those guys whose face you wanted to shove into the mud. Beating guys like him was wired into Matt's DNA.

"Well?"

Matt pulled his attention back to her hot question about his motivations. There was no way he wanted her to know the devastating effect she had on him… he refused to give her that much power.

But, sometimes, the truth, quietly stated, held more power than volatile accusations. "I'm not going to lie to you, Em. I'm attracted to you. And you're angry because you're attracted to me too."

"I gave you a chance to act on that attraction years ago, Matt, and you rejected me."

Interesting that she didn't bother to deny her attraction.

"I explained my reasons so stop throwing that in my face," Matt replied. "Get over it already."

As soon as the words left his mouth, he regretted them. He waited for her response, wondering whether he'd get a mouthful, a wobbly lip or, God forbid, tears.

Shame flickered in Emily's eyes. Matt watched, impressed, as she pushed starch into her spine and shoulders and held his stare. "You're right. It's over and it's not fair of me to keep tossing that back in your face."

Matt rubbed his jaw, shocked at her admission. Emily kept surprising him and he wasn't a man who was easily knocked off his stride. Fighting the urge to kiss her mouth, to pull her into his arms, he walked to the far end of the table where he'd left his half-full glass of water and quickly drained it. Keeping the table between them, he quietly thanked her for her apology before launching another verbal grenade. "I know that there's something fishy about your engagement to Morris."

"You don't know that—you don't know me!" Emily cried, throwing her hands up in the air.

Matt knew the smile he managed to pull onto his face was grim. "Maybe I don't know you but I do know him."

Nico was incapable of love, he wasn't the type. Matt knew this because it was all he and Morris had in common.

"Please just leave it alone, Matt," she begged.

He wished he could but he'd sooner be able to stop the world from turning. Rationally, he had no sane reason for inserting himself into her life—and his attraction to her didn't count. He'd been attracted to women in relationships before but his own moral code didn't allow him to move in on another man's territory.

He felt nothing for trying to poach Em away—Morris didn't deserve that much respect from him—but something else was bubbling between them. Something...

More.

Em was different, this situation was different and his spidey sense was clanging in his head. But, if he thought Em loved Morris, that she was genuinely into him, he'd walk away, respecting her choice. But deep down he knew love wasn't her motivation for marrying Morris so he wouldn't leave her alone.

Not yet anyway.

Matt ambled back over to her, bent down and briefly rested his lips on her temple. "Can't do that. I'll see you around, Em."

Matt was pretty sure he heard her release a small growl as he walked away but he knew his control was about to snap. If he turned around, he might just haul her into his arms and try a different way to persuade her to end this sham of an engagement.

At the meeting earlier in the week, Emily had agreed to give her new Brook Village fundraising committee members, two enthusiastic ladies who were new to Falling Brook, a tour of Davy's residential home. It was Saturday morning and the tour was over so the last person she expected to see approaching their table on the veranda of the intimate coffee shop was Matt Velez, looking far too sexy in a designer pair of soft-looking jeans, expensive athletic shoes and an untucked rich brown button-down shirt—sleeves rolled up muscled forearms—the exact color of his wonderful eyes.

Eyes that saw too much…

Emily looked down at her ripped-at-the-knees jeans, her off-the-shoulder black-and-white-striped sweater, and couldn't remember if she put on any makeup that morning. She'd been running late and was only expecting to meet Jane and Linda and not her pain-in-her-butt, make-my-heart-jump newest, and finest, committee member.

"Matt. I was *so* not expecting you." Emily said, placing her arm over the back of the chair. "And you're late so you missed the tour." Emily gestured to their empty coffee cups. "And we were all just leaving."

Matt ignored her belligerent tone and turned those soulful eyes onto her companions, his sexy mouth tipping up into a smile. "Morning, ladies, Em. Sorry I'm late."

He didn't give an excuse and Emily knew he'd deliberately timed his arrival to miss the tour. He wasn't there to find out more about Brook Village but to further his own agenda.

If only she knew what that was…

"Nico didn't join you this morning?" Matt asked, pulling out a chair and sitting down. Catching the eye of a waitress—Macy, one of the residents and Davy's good friend—he politely asked for coffee.

Macy, utterly flustered, giggled and skipped away. Emily sighed. Another conquest for Matt Velez.

After a few minutes of casual conversation, Jane and Linda rose and Matt, polite as always, shot to his feet. They said their goodbyes and Matt dropped down into his chair again, thanking Macy when she brought his cup.

"It's a good idea to have a small coffee shop on the premises, a place for the families to gather," Matt said, leaning back in his chair.

Yeah, it was great, except when her father chatted with *Russian mob bosses*! Emily looked around, saw many parents visiting the residents but couldn't see John, aka Ivan Sokolov. Come to think of it, he wasn't someone she often saw at Brook Village.

"Looking for someone?" Matt asked her.

Emily jerked her gaze back to him and shook her head. "No...*no.*"

Matt frowned at her overemphatic response. She could see the curiosity in his eyes so she spoke quickly to distract him. He was here, so talking about the facility seemed a safe topic for conversation.

"The residents each have their own living rooms and, depending on their abilities, they can provide their guests with refreshments or, if they want to, a meal," Emily explained. "Some of our residents have jobs but the coffee shop gives others the chance to earn some money on-site. The cooks are residents too."

"There's food?" Matt asked, sounding excited. "Great, I haven't had breakfast yet."

"I can recommend the food," Emily said. "Order the brie-and-cranberry toasted sandwich, it's divine."

Matt pulled a face and Emily smiled. "You really aren't an adventurous eater, are you?"

"Eggs and bacon will be just fine," Matt replied, his eyes steady on her face. "I'm adventurous in other areas."

His tone wasn't lecherous or salacious but Emily knew, just knew, he was referring to the bedroom. And boy, yeah, she could believe that. Matt would be a demanding lover, wringing every last drop of pleasure and pushing his partners to explore their sexuality. She'd had just two very unsatisfactory lovers and she was curious as to whether she could, actually, orgasm.

So far, the Big *O*s had been elusive. Some women, she'd read, never orgasmed at all and Em hoped, and prayed, that she didn't fall into that group. But, judging from the way Matt made her feel from just a few kisses—all hot and fluttery and off-balance—he might be the man to help her hit that particular target.

Damn him.

Matt's low laugh pulled her from the image of him taking her standing up, in a shower or against a wall, his hand under her thigh, pushing into her as he pinned her naked body against a hard surface. Yep, he'd make her come, she was pretty sure of it...

"I would donate a thousand dollars to Brook Village to know what you are thinking right now."

A thousand dollars? No way could she turn that

sort of money down. "I was thinking of you taking me up against a wall and the orgasm that followed."

Matt stared at her and Emily smiled at his initial shock at her bold words—yeah, she wasn't such a good girl after all! Then Matt's eyes flashed with interest and his cheeks darkened with heat. And, best of all, the hand holding his cup trembled. Good to know that she could knock the very smooth Matt Velez off his game.

"You can make the check out to the Brook Village," Emily told him.

"Done." Matt placed his coffee mug down and rested his forearms on the table. He stared at her and Emily couldn't look away; she'd never seen eyes so dark, holding a thousand secrets.

"But, for the record, those are not the sort of comments a happily engaged woman makes to another man, sweetheart. And it just reinforces my opinion that you're not happily engaged, Emily Arnott."

Ah, crap. This again.

He was too sharp, far too quick. Matt's brother, Juan, might be a genius but Matt had received more than his fair share of brains. Emily forced herself to act casual.

"I'm engaged, not dead, Matteo. And it would be disingenuous of me to deny I am attracted to you since we kissed the other night." She wiggled her fingers of her left hand, pulling her attention to her ring. "But I am engaged. To Nico."

She really had to work on sounding more enthusiastic.

Emily wanted to know why he was so against her marrying Nico. Why did he keep pushing and prying; why did he care? Oh, she knew he desired her—their lava-hot kiss earlier in the week proved that—but if sex was all he was after, then she knew there was no shortage of candidates to share his bed. Around him, women fell like pins in a bowling alley, unable to resist his bad-boy-made-good looks and cocky attitude.

"And this has got me wondering…" Emily said, tapping her index finger on the glass tabletop.

"About?" Matt asked, back to looking cool and collected.

"What's your beef with…" she couldn't push the word *fiancé* past her lips "…with Nico? And don't tell me you don't have one," she added.

No, Matt Velez had an agenda and it had more to do with her fiancé and less to do with her. Matt had a problem with Morris; that much was obvious.

But did the root cause of his hostility matter? Did she care as long as his animosity toward Nico benefited her? On one level, it would make sense to team up with him, both of them working to take Nico down—she was pretty sure Matt would be happy to trample on any and all of Nico's dreams and he might even have information on Nico she could use.

But she couldn't take the chance of letting him in on her secret. Gina was the only person she'd told and that was because she told Gina everything. And Gina was trying to source information on Nico to help her break her engagement, desperately flipping over rocks to find something to get Nico to leave her alone. She trusted Gina with her life.

She didn't trust Matt. Nobody could know about Nico's bizarre but exceedingly effective scheme. He'd identified what was most important to her dad and to her, Arnott's reputation, and he'd pushed her between a rock and a concrete pillar.

She had to resolve this issue fast. She would not risk Arnott's: her dad lost his wife when Vernon Lowell ran away with his and his clients' money, and Arnott's was now her dad's refuge and his true love.

He wasn't a great dad, probably wasn't even a good one, but he was hers and she had to protect him, protect their name and the source of their income.

And keep Nico at a distance until she had the dirt she needed to force him to leave her alone. Because there was dirt, of this she was certain.

Matt was saved from having to respond to her question when arms encircled her neck and a masculine jaw rubbed her cheek. She recognized the scent of Davy's soap and pushed her way to her feet, turning to hug her big brother.

After a minute, maybe two—Davy was super affectionate and loved to hug—Emily pulled back and gripped his shoulders. "Davy. How was your week, honey?"

"Angel! You're here. I'm so happy to see you!" Davy responded. "And my week was good."

His curious eyes, the same purple-blue shade as hers, bounced between her and Matt.

"Who's he?" Davy whispered. "He needs a haircut but I do like his watch."

Emily saw Matt's mouth twitching and knew that Matt had heard his not-so-quiet words. Matt, to her surprise, held out his hand for Davy to shake. "I'm Matt. And you're right, I do need a haircut."

Matt released Davy's hand and gestured him to the spare seat next to Emily. "Take a seat, Davy. I'm about to have breakfast. Would you like to join me?"

Davy sat down and nodded. "I always have pancakes on Saturday."

"Are the pancakes good?" Matt asked.

Emily was impressed by Matt's easy way of talking, his open expression. So many people talked down, or slowly, to people with special needs, and more than a few were openly patronizing. Matt, bless him, just acted normally.

"So good. I like mine with bananas and peanut butter," Davy told him.

"I see you and your brother share a love for bizarre food combinations," Matt said to Emily, wincing at the thought.

Emily couldn't help her grin. "Try it—I dare you."

"And what will you reward me if I do?" Matt asked, amusement in his eyes.

Emily's eyes dropped to his mouth and she knew what he wanted. And damn, she craved that too but she couldn't go there. Not now.

Probably never. A weight settled on her heart as the thought grew bigger and bigger in her head. He wasn't the man for her, could never be the man for her. Not now because she was temporarily engaged and not later because she couldn't risk loving another person and having him leave her. Once was more than enough.

She'd never put herself in that position again.

"My reward, Em?" Matt prompted her.

Oh, right. "I'll pay for your breakfast," she said, wishing she could tell him that what she really wanted was to be in his arms, to feel the rough scrape of his stubble against her skin, feel overwhelmed by his kisses.

"That's not what you really wanted to say."

Of course it wasn't, but there was no way she'd ever admit that to him. She was already neck deep; she didn't need to hasten her drowning.

Davy clapped his hands and Emily looked at him, then smiled at his beaming face. She turned to see who'd caught her brother's attention and saw that it was Macy, who was approaching their table, intent on filling up Matt's cup. It didn't escape her attention that all of Macy's attention was directed to Matt and Emily had yet to be offered coffee.

Macy looked at Matt, blushed and rocked from foot to foot. "Do you want more coffee?" Macy asked Matt.

Matt shook his head. "Thank you, Macy, I've had enough. But I'm sure Emily would like a refill."

Emily felt a jolt of pleasure at his thoughtful gesture. "Thanks, Macy, that would be good. And could you ask the kitchen to bring us two plates of pancakes?" Emily arched her brows at Matt, openly challenging him. "Bananas and peanut butter?"

Matt pulled a face but didn't, to his credit, back down. "Yes, bananas and peanut butter."

"Brave boy," Emily murmured.

"Payback will be fun," Matt told her, his eyes suggesting that he'd like to take his revenge when she was naked and panting. Emily couldn't stop herself from blushing, wishing she didn't want that so damn much.

Because, really, life was complicated enough as it was...

Matt thanked Macy again before turning his attention back to Davy. He leaned across the table and tapped his finger against the dial of Davy's watch. "I like your watch too, Davy. It's pretty special. Where did you get it?"

Emily listened as Davy explained that his vintage Rolex was their grandfather's, how his dad passed it to him when he turned twenty-one. "It's not as fancy as yours, Matt—it doesn't have as many buttons or numbers."

Matt shook his head, not breaking eye contact with her brother. "But mine is new—it never belonged to my grandfather. That's a pretty special thing."

"Did you know your granddaddy?"

Emily saw pain flash in Matt's eyes and saw his lips tighten. She waited for his reply, half expecting him to deflect Davy's curious question. "No, I didn't."

Four words but they were infused with pain. Emily wanted to place a reassuring hand on Matt's, to squeeze his arm. But she resisted the impulse. Matt was a proud man and wouldn't appreciate the gesture. But, from the pain flashing in his eyes and the four words, she realized his relationship with his family wasn't good. She sympathized; she wasn't on any terms with her mom and knew how much it stung to be estranged from a parent.

"Do you play foosball, Matt? Angel and I always play foosball in the rec room. I kick her butt."

Emily couldn't let that falsehood go unchallenged. "Davy Arnott, you know that's not true. I beat you more often than not." Keeping her finger in the air, she pointed it in Matt's direction. "And Davy is the only person, ever, who gets to call me Angel."

"I wouldn't dream of it," Matt smoothly replied. "Besides, you're more of an imp than an angel."

Emily grinned at him. That was one of the best compliments she'd ever received.

Matt's lips curved and Emily felt her stomach flip over and wondered when the few butterflies in her stomach turned into a swarm.

Matt turned his attention to Davy. "After breakfast, I'll play foosball with you. And, if you like, I'll whip your angel's butt for you."

Matt met her annoyed glance with another of his devastating smiles. "Stand down, imp, I called you *his* angel. And here comes Macy with our pancakes. And can I just ask, what exactly is wrong with bacon and maple syrup?"

She got her butt kicked at foosball. Davy, inspired by Matt's take-no-prisoners policy, beat her by a few

goals and then Matt thoroughly trounced her, much
to Davy's delight.

Nico, Emily couldn't help thinking as she walked
at Matt's side to their respective cars in the parking
lot, hadn't even bothered to talk to Davy. A strange
attitude since he was going to be the guy's brother-in-
law. In fact, this whole engagement was super strange;
Nico, apart from a few text messages, hadn't made
contact with her since his proposal—could you call a
blackmail demand a proposal?—nearly ten days ago.

She wasn't complaining but it was weird…

"Your brother is a trip."

Emily smiled at his words. "I'm sure playing foosball isn't how you spend most of your Saturday morn-
ings."

"No, I normally spend my morning at my computer catching up on everything I didn't get to during the week. This was a nice change of pace," Matt
replied. "I had as much fun as he did—it was nice to
have some fun and easy company."

Emily, her bag over her shoulder, tucked her hands
in the back pockets of her jeans. She'd enjoyed her
morning far more than expected; it had been a nice
change of pace for her too. And, let's be honest here,
she never expected Matt Velez to be the type to play
foosball with not only Davy, but some of the other
guys in the rec room. They'd invited him to play bas-
ketball with them and he said he couldn't but that he'd
be back to kick their asses.

His easy, normal ribbing delighted Davy and his
friends. Of course, she didn't expect him to return to

Brook Village—he was a busy guy with a demanding career—but he'd brightened their morning and for that, Emily was grateful.

"You're obviously committed to this place—how long have you been sitting on the fundraising committee?" Matt commented.

"I've been sitting as a trustee on their board for a couple of years and took over the fundraising portfolio a few years ago."

"You were about ten percent short of your fundraising goal last year—are you planning anything else to make up that shortfall?"

He really had done his homework. Matt, as she was coming to accept, wasn't only sexy, hot and ripped but he was also full of surprises.

"I'd love to do more but with my work and my—" Emily hesitated, looking for the right words"—with Nico, I haven't really given it much thought. I'm not sure I have the time to plan anything else."

And she still had to start on her quest for information on Nico. She had no idea where to start. That had to go to the top of her priority list. She'd start trawling the internet for information on her fiancé when she got home, maybe look into what a private investigator charged. If she could find one who was affordable and discreet, hiring him, or her, might be an option.

Maybe she could tell the PI that she wanted some background information on her reticent fiancé, wanted to know more about him before she committed herself to this man.

That sounded reasonable, didn't it?

Matt placed his hand on Emily's forearm, his big hand easily wrapping around it. "You keep doing that."

"Doing what?" Emily asked, trying to ignore her sizzling skin.

"You, mentally, wander off. I can easily see when you are miles away."

Emily sighed. "I have a lot on my mind, Matt."

"I know that." Matt lifted his hand and rubbed his thumb over her bottom lip and Emily wished he'd kiss her. Then she remembered that she was technically, albeit reluctantly, engaged and wasn't allowed to kiss other men.

This engagement really wasn't working for her. In a lot of ways...

"Do me a favor, imp?"

She so loved him calling her that. She shouldn't but she did. "What?"

"If and when you decide you are out of your depth, call me." Matt's hand dropped to her hip and, before she could complain, he snagged her phone from the back pocket of her jeans. Ignoring her attempt to snatch it from him, he slid his thumb across the screen and grinned when the phone opened.

"No passcode or thumbprint? You're not very security conscious, Arnott."

"It's a phone, not nuclear codes." Emily retorted. "And what are you doing with it?"

"Putting my number in your contacts." Matt tapped the screen a few times before handing it back to her. Then his expression turned serious, and Emily saw the worry in his eyes. "Seriously, Em, call me. Call me anytime."

It was so tempting but the risk was too great. Emily snatched her phone back and held it in a tight grip. "I keep telling you—I'm *fine*, Velez."

Matt tapped her nose. "Thousands might believe you, my sexy imp, but, unfortunately for you, I don't."

Matt hit a button on his remote and a beautiful two-door Mercedes responded with a quiet whoop and the flash of pretty lights. Oh, she did like his car. It's long svelte hood and curvaceous lines made it instantly recognizable. "It's the new AMG GT C Roadster."

Matt's eyebrows rose. "It is. I only got it recently and I'm enjoying it. Do you like cars?"

"No, I *love* cars," Emily said, walking over to the gorgeous vehicle and running her hand over its smooth hood. "She's beautiful. And dangerous."

Emily felt Matt stop behind her, so close she could feel the heat radiating off him, smell his sex-and-soap scent. Why did he always have to smell so damn good?

"I like beautiful and dangerous," Matt said, his knuckles running down the center of her back, stopping at the tip of her butt. He leaned forward and when he spoke, Emily felt his breath on the shell of her ear and his words deep inside her. "Maybe that's why I like you."

The residents of Falling Brook, most of whom knew her from the time she wore pigtails, saw her as being polite and hardworking, conscientious and as somebody who tried hard not to put a foot wrong or rock the boat.

She didn't do drugs, smoke or sleep around but the fact that Matt saw her differently thrilled her.

Matt stepped away from her, opened his car door and slid inside. He hit the start button and the engine turned, raucous and cheeky. The driver's window slid down silently and Matt nodded at her phone before pinning her with a hard look. "Don't hesitate to call me, imp."

Emily needed to say something, anything. "I'm very independent and I don't rely on anybody for anything."

"Then why are you getting married, Emily?"

Damn, she'd walked straight into that. Because he'd backed her into a corner, Emily went on the offensive. "If I was a guy, would you be saying the same thing?" Emily challenged him.

"No, because you're not a guy, you're a woman I want and can't have." Matt pushed both hands into his hair, obviously frustrated. "And that's wrong on so many levels."

"Not used to being thwarted?" Emily taunted him.

"I always get what I want. Eventually." Matt nodded at her phone still in her hands. "At the risk of repeating myself, call me. For anything…"

Emily raised her eyebrows, unable to stop herself from flushing. Anything? Anything at all? And, yes, she was tempted.

Not that she'd ever, ever admit that to him.

Five

Emily pushed her salad leaves around her plate, idly thinking that time dragged when you weren't having fun. Nico had called her shortly after she returned from Brook Village and told her he was back in town and that they were going to dinner at L'Albri, a fine, French-inspired restaurant situated on the main street in town. It was a see-and-be-seen restaurant, upmarket and very snobby.

Emily hated the food, the small portions, the supercilious waiters and the sheer pretentiousness of the place. She'd far prefer to be eating a burger down the road at Al's Diner but Emily knew that Nico would rather die than be seen at the real, homey and down-to-earth eatery.

Soon after finishing his fish dish, Nico had excused himself to talk to a potential client across the room and left her alone at the table. That had been twenty-five minutes ago. He'd interrupted a private dinner and Emily could see the frustration on their trying-to-be-polite faces.

Unlike Matt, Nico had no idea about social cues.

She had to stop thinking about Matt Velez, comparing him to Nico. But she couldn't help it; they were complete opposites. Matt's hair was dark and unruly, he was olive-skinned and his dark eyes radiated intelligence.

Nico kept pushing his limp, dishwater-blond hair out of his cold, light, malicious eyes, and while he could be good looking if he smiled, he rarely did.

Like all women her age, she enjoyed a guy's good looks but she wasn't that shallow that looks were the beginning and end of everything. Nico would be nice looking if he wasn't a scum-sucking extortionist intent on blackmailing her into marriage.

Emily pushed her coffee cup away and, looking toward the front of the restaurant, smiled when she saw Gina standing at the concierge's table. Waving her over, she grinned when her friend dropped into the chair Nico vacated.

"Are you meeting someone?" Emily asked, happy to see her friend and to have some company.

"In ten minutes or so—you know that I like to get here early," Gina replied.

"To see if he's cute or not. If he isn't you send him a text message claiming stomach flu," Emily gently chided her.

Gina shrugged, unperturbed. "What's the point in spending time with someone you aren't, and could never be, attracted to?"

Then she added, sotto voce, "Unless you're being blackmailed…"

"Thanks for the reminder."

"Since you're not going to finish this, may I?" Gina asked, pointing to Emily's wineglass. When Emily nodded, Gina picked it up and took a healthy sip from her half-full glass. "How was dinner?"

"Interminable," Emily admitted. "I've spent most of the evening imagining stabbing him with my fork."

Emily tapped the table with her index finger. "Somehow Nico heard that Matt joined my fundraising committee and he warned me off him."

Gina grimaced. "Yeah, they don't like each other at all."

"Matt and Nico?"

Gina slowly nodded. "Nico worked at MJR Investing and the rumor is that he and Matt were at loggerheads all the time. Like…one said blue, the other would say pink. They were also super competitive. But that's just second- or third-hand gossip—I'm trying to find a direct source." She paused, and then asked, "So what did you tell Nico about Matt?"

"I picked my words carefully, reminding him that Matt is an influential businessman and that I'm grateful he's giving Brook Village his support. He called me naive, telling me that Matt never does anything out of the goodness of his heart."

"And do you think that's true?"

She did, actually; Gina's earlier words about Matt being competitive rang true. Matt wanted her and Emily wasn't sure that he'd want her quite as much if she wasn't engaged to Nico. Matt liked to win and Emily felt a little like a bone two dogs wanted. Sure, he was attracted to her, but she doubted he'd be pursuing her quite so ardently if Nico wasn't in the picture.

"I like Matt, far more than I like Nico but, as per Falling Brook gossip," Gina told her, keeping her voice low, "Matt got the CEO job Nico wanted and he's still bitter about it."

"That was years ago."

"Nico is also very well-known for holding a grudge. Like, it's his *thing*," Gina whispered. "And he never backs down from a challenge. So, did you piss him off or challenge him, Em?"

Emily darted a look a Nico before lifting and dropping her hands. "We went on a couple of dates—I told him I wasn't going to sleep with him and that there wasn't any chemistry. That he wasn't my type."

Gina clicked her fingers and pointed her index finger at Emily's chest. "Apparently he thinks he's everybody's type and he likes to be the one to break it off. So, there you go, a motive for the current madness. And when you add Matt to the madness…"

Emily scowled at her. "What does that mean?"

"Oh, please, the sparks fly when you two are together. I feel like I need to wear a fire-retardant suit," Gina scoffed.

"He's a good-looking guy," Emily said, keeping her tone neutral.

"Honey, that's like calling a NASA space shuttle a toy rocket. The man is superfine." Gina twisted her lips. "Though admittedly, as much as I like him, it is weird that he's back in your life as soon as you get engaged."

"Temporarily engaged," Emily corrected her. And yes, the thought about Matt's timing had occurred. Like Gina, she didn't know what to make of Matt's attention.

Emily noticed that Nico was now on his feet and she leaned back, putting a polite look on her face. She subtly gestured to Gina to end their conversation.

Gina frowned at her. "For God's sake, Em, get yourself out of this mess."

"I'm trying," Emily retorted, her voice low enough for only Gina to hear. As Nico approached, Gina stood up, draped her bag over her shoulder and sent Nico the fakest of fake smiles.

"My date has just arrived. And he's quite cute…"

Gina walked away before she had to interact with Nico. When Nico reached the table and sat down, he picked up the leather folder the waiter left earlier with the bill tucked inside and handed it to Emily. "Your turn to pay, my dear."

Emily opened her mouth to argue but caught Nico's narrow-eyed gaze. He was waiting for her to disagree, hoping she'd argue. Emily pulled a smile on her face and quickly nodded.

"Sure."

She opened the folder and winced when she saw that the bill for his potential client had been added to their bill. She picked it up and handed it to Nico. "They've charged us for their meals and drinks."

"I'm going to meet them in Chicago next week when I attend the weeklong investment conference. To say thank you, I offered to pay for their meal," Nico replied.

But why did she have to pay for it? On what planet was that fair?

"Is there a problem, Emily?" Nico asked, his voice silky smooth.

Emily opened her mouth to reply but held back the words. If she started, they'd be here all night.

Midmorning on Monday, Emily looked up at the sound of a light rap on her door and saw Matt standing in her open doorway, his shoulder against the frame, dressed in fawn-colored chinos, a sky blue shirt and a nut-brown jacket.

She loved his style; he always looked good and never gave the impression he'd spent hours in front of a mirror planning his outfit.

Emily gave herself a moment to enjoy the view of a tall, masculine, hot guy standing in her doorway. But she knew she was playing with fire; if Nico found out that Matt was making unscheduled appearances at her office, he'd lose it.

It made her throat sting and her stomach cramp but she needed to keep Nico, for the time being at least, happy.

Fear, and the fact that Matt caused her skin to tingle and her heart rate to climb, made Emily's voice sharper and harder than she intended. "Why are you here? And I thought I employed a PA to guard my door."

Matt straightened, stepped into her office and closed the door behind him. After walking over to her desk, he placed his hands on the surface and leaned toward her, his expression intense.

"Are you okay?"

No, she was exhausted and stressed and anxiety was eating a hole in her stomach. No one but him had noticed and Emily lifted her hands in a gesture of confusion. Why did he keep seeing what she most wanted to keep hidden?

"What's wrong, imp?"

Emily desperately wished he was someone she could confide in but she couldn't afford to. She was on her own here. "Nothing is wrong—I'm just busy and you're interrupting my morning."

"Liar," Matt whipped back. "The shadows are deeper under your eyes and your fingers are trembling."

Emily looked down at her hands and yep, he was right, her fingers were bouncing up and down. And she hadn't slept or eaten much in the last thirty-six hours.

Dealing with Nico was like fighting a particularly nasty virus.

How wonderful it would be just to hand this over to Matt or even to talk through her options with him but she couldn't. Nico was too volatile and she didn't know Matt well enough to trust that he'd keep her secret. She'd trusted people before—her Mom to stay, her dad to connect with her—and they'd all, in one way or another, let her down.

The stakes were too high for her to take a gamble on Matt Velez.

No, she was on her own.

Emily gestured to the monitor on her desk. "I'm busy, Matt. What do you want?"

Matt straightened before moving around to sit on her side of the desk. He stretched out his long legs, folded his arms across his chest and his biceps strained the seams of the expensive fabric.

So hot... *Concentrate, Emily.*

Matt raked a frustrated hand through his hair and sighed. "For someone who looks like butter wouldn't melt in her mouth, you are more stubborn than a pack of mules. As for why I'm here...do you remember I gave Davy my cell number on Saturday?"

"Yeah?"

"He called me about forty minutes ago...and he's fine, Em."

Words to cool her blood. Emily shot to her feet, terror galloping through her system. "What happened? Where is he? Is he hurt?"

Matt placed both his hands on her shoulders and gently pushed her back into her chair. "He's fine. He was well enough to call me, remember?"

"What. Happened?"

"He got into a fight."

Emily shot to her feet again. "What the actual hell?"

A small smile touched Matt's face. "When I say fight, it was more of a scuffle, with minor injuries. Davy has a split lip. The other guy has a bloody nose. I think he was quite proud of his injuries and that's why he called me."

What was happening in her life? Her brother didn't get into fights, she wasn't sexually frustrated, normality didn't include being blackmailed into marriage and her brother didn't call virtual strangers when he got into trouble, he called her!

"Breathe, Em," Matt told her, pulling her to stand between his spread legs, his hands resting lightly on her waist.

Emily pulled in some air, held it for a couple of beats and pushed it out. She repeated the action a few times before her head stopped whirling. When she felt a little calmer, she placed her hands on Matt's biceps and looked up into his surprisingly gentle eyes. He grounded her, she realized. Just being next to him made her feel calmer and stronger and more resilient. He filled her up…

Pity she couldn't explore these new and strange feelings and the attraction bubbling and boiling between them.

Matt placed his hand on her cheek and swiped his thumb across her cheekbone. "Better?"

Emily nodded. "Davy got into a fight?" She couldn't believe it.

Matt nodded. "According to a staff member, some new guy was teasing another guy, Davy told him to knock it off, he wouldn't. Davy pushed him, new guy punched Davy, Davy smacked him back and the staff intervened."

Holy crap.

"He didn't want you fussing and it wasn't that big a deal. It was just a little scuffle." Matt moved his hand down her cheek to her neck and her shoulders, his strong fingers digging into the tight muscles of her shoulders. "Honey, you're so tense. You've got to learn to relax…"

"Relax? Are you kidding me? I have an absent mother, a father who is addicted to his work, a brother who is getting into fights and a fiancé who is bla—"

Emily snapped her jaw closed, horrified that she'd nearly let her secret slip. Oh God, she was so tired and so stressed and she didn't know if she could take much more. It was all too much.

Emily tried to swallow down her tears but they welled and she softly cursed when a couple rolled down her cheeks. Dammit, if she didn't manage to get herself under control, she might just throw herself on Matt's chest and weep for days.

Emily waved her hands in front of her face to dry her wet eyes. "Sorry. I'm a mess."

Matt captured a tear on his thumb. "You are."

Emily snorted. "Thanks." Leaning past him, she grabbed a tissue from the box on her desk and dabbed her eyes, hoping her mascara lived up to its claim of being waterproof. Looking like a raccoon would just be a step too far.

Emily pulled in a deep breath, then another. "Okay, better."

Stepping out from between Matt's legs, she picked up her bag and placed it on the table. Talking to herself, she pulled out her sunglasses, her car keys and tapped her keyboard to shut down her computer. "Gina can cancel my appointments for the rest of the day and I'll spend the afternoon with Davy at Brook Village."

Matt plucked her car keys out of her hand. "I'll drive you. Davy asked me to swing by so we'll go together."

It wasn't a good idea and Nico might find out. Emily shook her head and held out her hand for her keys. She had to do this alone…

Matt kept her keys in his hand. "What's the problem, Em?"

Humiliation washed over her. "Nico…" She couldn't say more, couldn't explain. She wanted to be with Matt but she was terrified Nico would find out. She was acting like a woman having an affair and she didn't like it but what choice did she have?

"Morris left for Chicago this morning so, unless he has a GPS tracker on your phone or car, he won't be able to track your movements," Matt briskly told her. Before she could ask how he knew what Nico's movements were, he took her hand and interlinked their fingers.

"Let's go, imp, daylight's wasting."

Matt knew Morris was in Chicago because he followed him on Instagram under a fake name and the D-bag had posted a selfie of himself checking into the hotel where the conference was being held. Like Nico, Matt registered to attend, booked his room and his flight and canceled none of his arrangements.

He needed Nico to think that he was in Chicago, somewhere amongst the two thousand delegates. It gave him a little room to move, some time to persuade Emily to trust him.

Years ago he'd said she was a guppy amongst sharks, but this time around she was swimming with a great white and Matt was terrified she was going to be eaten alive.

Matt looked at Emily sitting in the passenger seat of his low-to-the-ground Roadster. He'd bundled her into his car, telling her that he'd drive and, to his surprise, she hadn't put up much of an argument, telling him exactly how stressed she was. Matt looked at her profile again, thinking that she looked younger than her years today and utterly exhausted. She needed a break and he intended to give her one.

It took another ten minutes for Emily to realize that they weren't on the right road to Brook Village. "Why are we heading toward the freeway?" she demanded. "We're supposed to be going to Brook Village."

"Not happening," Matt replied, sending her a lazy smile.

"I am going to see my brother," Emily stated, sounding pissed. "Turn this car around."

Matt patted her thigh and felt her stiffen. She didn't like being ordered about and he liked that she wasn't a pushover. He couldn't abide women who didn't push back.

And that was why he knew that something was very wrong with her engagement to Morris; he was the ultimate control freak and possessive as hell. Emily didn't like being told what to do and control was Nico's favorite thing so there had to be another reason why they were together...

Their engagement wasn't about affection or love. And, judging by the way she'd kissed him, it wasn't about passion either. Something else was making her act out of character. And he desperately wanted to know what that was but, until she opened up, he couldn't help her.

And that pissed him off.

Jealously and envy might've been his initial motivation when he'd first found out about her engagement; he couldn't tolerate the thought of Morris having someone he so desperately wanted. Matt felt a wave of shame; he wasn't proud he'd let his ego override his mind.

But, lately, he'd come to sense, to know, that something was very wrong with this scenario and he was becoming increasingly worried about Emily. He felt protective and concerned and, along with craving her constantly, was desperate for her to confide in him.

But the more he pushed, the further she retreated.

"Your brother doesn't need you rushing to check on his injuries. He's embarrassed and remorseful—he needs time to work through what he did and the implications of his actions by himself, for himself," Matt gently suggested. "Give the guy some space, Em."

"You don't understand, Matt, he's—"

"He's a *guy*, and he still has his pride. Give him some space, a little time. Later this evening, give him a call but don't harp on what happened. The staff has it in hand."

Matt knew that Emily wanted to disagree with him and that she was trying to find something to say to counter his argument. When she released a sharp huff, he knew that he'd won this round.

"So, if we're not going to Brook Village then you might as well take me back to the office."

Ding, ding, ding, there went the bell to commence round two. "Nope. You need a break and you've already canceled your appointments for the day, as have I, and we're going to play hooky. When last did you do something unexpected?"

He'd bet today's profits, and they'd been substantial, that Emily didn't take time off from her responsibilities, which were heavier than he'd imagined.

She needed some time away, a few hours of down time, and he was going to make sure she relaxed. Of course, he knew of one or two other activities that would take her mind off her problems but the chances of getting her naked were minuscule.

Less than that…

Sadly.

"Matt…"

"Em," Matt replied, humor in his voice. Approaching a traffic light, he braked as the light changed and when he brought the Roadster to a stop, he turned to look into her obstinate, adorable face.

"Imp, just let go, okay? Davy is fine—he doesn't

need or want you around today. On our way back in, I'll check on him." When Emily started to speak, Matt shook his head. "It's a beautiful day so I thought we'd drive to Montauk. You can walk barefoot in the sand, listen to the waves—I won't even talk if you don't want me to."

Emily raised a skeptical eyebrow and Matt grinned.

"I'll try not to talk," Matt amended. He lifted his hand and squeezed her shoulder, her muscles tight beneath his fingertips. "You need a day to unwind, to de-stress. The world won't stop if you take some downtime."

"It might," Emily stated, sounding grumpy.

"I promise it won't." Matt noticed the light changing and accelerated away. "We're about to hit the highway—do you want to go back or should I keep driving?"

If she said she wanted to return to work he'd take her, of course he would. Unlike her fiancé, he didn't back women into corners, bully or coerce them into a course of action.

He was an alpha male, bossy as hell, but not, he hoped, a jerk.

"Drive on, Velez. I don't have the energy to argue with you."

Matt grinned, smart enough to take her grumpy statement for the capitulation it was.

Six

Matt, returning from the bathroom at the beachfront restaurant, looked across the near empty eatery on the outskirts of Montauk to see Emily sitting at their small table outside, her chin in the palm of her hand and her eyes on a ship sitting on the horizon.

Longing whispered through him and his normally unflappable heart bounced off his ribcage. He was gut-wrenchingly, toe-curlingly attracted to Emily, on a deep and fundamental level. Sure, she was beautiful; it was hard to miss that but, strangely, her looks weren't that big a deal anymore. His attraction to her went deeper than the surface and, while her beauty still gut punched him occasionally, it was the little things about her that now intrigued him.

The three freckles in perfect alignment on the side

of her neck; her preposterously long and dark eye-lashes; her elegant fingers he longed to feel sliding over his skin.

He'd also started to look past her outer layer into what made Emily and he liked what he saw. She was a little sassy, smart and, occasionally, funny.

And yeah, his attraction to Emily no longer had anything to do with wanting what he thought Nico had.

No, his need and desire for Emily was a living, breathing entity.

It simply *was*. Hot, demanding, hard to ignore.

Matt resumed his walk and stepped onto the deck. When he reached their table, he placed his hand on the back of her head and dropped his lips to hers, un-able to resist taking a quick taste, to hear that sharp intake of breath, to feel her lips soften under his.

What was supposed to be a brief peck turned deeper and darker. Em's arm came up to curl around his neck and she grabbed the fabric of his shirt with her other hand, twisting it in her fist as her mouth opened to his.

He couldn't resist; he didn't *want* to resist. Matt held her face in both his hands as his tongue swept into her mouth. She tasted liked strawberry-flavored lip gloss, the lemonade she was drinking, of heaven and hell. Heaven because he could stand here, at this odd angle for the rest of his life just kissing her. And hell because he knew that at any moment she'd return to her senses and push him away.

He felt her stiffen, her tongue retreating from his… three, two, one…

Yep, and she was gone.

Matt dropped a kiss on the top of her head before taking the seat opposite her, waiting for her to look at him. When she did, Emily showed him the back of her left hand and the god-awful diamond she sported on her ring finger. "Engaged, remember?"

"You don't kiss like you are," Matt retorted, frustrated.

Emily twisted her head to look inside the restaurant, to see if anyone was watching them. He caught the panic and fear in her eyes and that just pissed him off. "The only other customers are three old guys at the bar who are playing cards. Relax, for God's sake," he told her, his tone terse.

Emily faced forward again and gripped the sides of her head with both hands. "You're not helping, Matteo."

Matt tipped his face to the sun and looked at the blue sky above. He could argue with her, tell her that he knew she didn't love Morris and demand to know why she was engaged. Honestly, if he could shake the truth out of her, he would.

But it wasn't curiosity driving him, or his innate need to be the best; he just wanted to help Emily because he was damn sure she needed it.

For the first time ever, Matt wanted to take on someone else's fight. But he couldn't, not until she opened up and let him in. Matt was coming to understand that Em was scared but she was also stubborn. He wouldn't get anywhere by pushing her.

A waitress approached them, told them about the catch of the day and reassured them that the restaurant was famous for their seafood and that, over weekends, tables were hard to come by. When the waitress walked away with their orders, Matt leaned back and linked his hands over his flat stomach.

"Tell me about Arnott's."

Emily pushed a long, pale strand of hair out of her eyes but the wind just blew it back. Emily dug into her bag, pulled out a band and quickly and efficiently pulled her hair off her face and into a rough knot at the back of her head. Gorgeous.

"That's a broad question—what would you like to know?"

"Tell me how you got into looking after managing your clients with special needs," Matt clarified his question.

"Ah." Emily half turned in her chair and crossed her legs, her shoe dangling off the top of her foot. "Well, Davy is four years older than me and when he turned eighteen, he moved into Brook Village. Dad's small financial services company was doing quite well back then because, as you gathered, the residential village is not cheap."

He'd looked up their fees online, *not cheap* was an understatement.

"Davy loved it but, six months after he started living there, Dad lost most of his money when Black Crescent crashed. I was fourteen at the time."

So many people had been impacted by Vernon Lowell's actions but Matt hadn't realized the Arnotts were one of the families that had been affected. "Your dad is an investor himself—why did he put his money into Black Crescent?"

Emily stared out to sea, obviously debating how much to say. "Vernon Lowell and my dad were good friends back in the day. My dad knows the mechanics of buying and selling but he has no instinct for trading. He only ever buys safe, solid stocks, small gains over the long term. He admired Vernon's verve and willingness to take a risk and he invested a little money with him and it earned a huge return. Then he invested more and more until all his savings were tied up in Black Crescent. Then Lowell disappeared and so did all his investors' cash."

It was a story Matt had heard so many times before.

Emily's eyes fogged over with pain. "My mom left shortly after Black Crescent crashed and my dad sank into a deep depression. Eventually, he pulled himself out of the fog and started to run the business again but Davy and I lost him to his work."

"And you felt abandoned. For the second time."

Emily nodded. "You're very astute and yes, I did. I've never felt so alone as I did for those six months. It wasn't a great time."

Matt knew what it felt like to feel alone. He'd lived that way most of his life. "I understand that more than you know. And your mom? Do you have any contact with her?" Matt asked.

"I went to see her after she left. I caught a bus, traveled for six hours. I got to her new place, rang the doorbell and she bundled me into her car and drove me straight back to the bus station. She told me that it was my job to look after my dad and Davy, that she'd done it for long enough and she deserved a normal family."

"Jesus."

"It really confirmed what I always suspected, that she didn't love me or want us. Then again, I did have a hint of what she was going to do when I was eight," Emily said, her voice flat and emotionless. "I knew she was going to leave me...leave us. God, I don't know why I'm telling you this—I don't generally rake up the past."

Matt ignored that comment, curious as to why so young a child would suspect her mother was going to leave. "How did you know that?"

Emily answered his gentle question. "We were in a shop and I needed shoes, or a jacket, something for school," Emily told him, drawing patterns on the wooden table with her thumbnail. "I wanted to look at a toy, or something, told her that I'd be right back, asked her if she'd wait for me and kept asking for reassurance that she'd be where I left her."

"And she wasn't."

Emily's eyes deepened with pain. "They found me somewhere in the store, crying. I remember looking for her but not finding her. They took me home and she was there and she told the authorities that she was on her way to the police to report me missing. I knew that to be a lie."

"Did you tell your dad?"

"She told me not to, that my dad would be mad at me and wouldn't love me anymore if I tattled on her."

Matt's mouth dropped open. "*What?* God, Em."

"I know it happened a long time ago but, to this day, I'll still do anything not to upset him." Emily tried to smile. "I sense that you didn't have a great relationship with your dad," Emily said, turning the spotlight on him.

"With either of my parents," Matt quietly answered her, wondering why he was discussing his past with Emily when he never discussed his family with anyone. Ever. But she'd opened up so he should reciprocate, just a little. His estranged relationship with his parents and brother was an open secret and, while she was the first person he'd discuss his past with, it didn't mean anything more than friendship. And telling her wouldn't hurt...

"They were all about Juan—"

"Your brilliant older brother." Emily placed her chin in the palm of her hand, her eyes steady on his face. "Is he why you became Falling Brook's greatest rebel?"

"Everything in our house revolved around Juan. I spent a lot of my childhood and teens looking for attention, the good, bad and ugly," Matt admitted. "I finally grew out of acting like an ass when I went to college."

"Do you have a relationship with them now?" Emily asked, her voice soft.

Matt shook his head. "We speak every six months, exchange awkward calls at Christmas and on birthdays. Do you talk to your mom?"

"No, she threw herself into being the mother to the daughters of the man she left my father for." Emily's mouth flattened in pain. "I never understood how she could just walk away and replace me. But she did."

Matt knew that if he offered any comfort, the spell between them would be broken and Em would clam up. So instead of offering empty platitudes, he just kept his eyes on her, his expression empathetic but holding no pity. He loathed pity and suspected that Emily did too.

A strand of that blond-white hair blew across her eyes, defied the knot and Emily tucked it behind her ear. She looked away and when she spoke again, Matt knew that the door to her soul was firmly latched. "So, I wonder if the rumors about Joshua Lowell's love child are true?"

It was a hell of a change of subject. "We overheard him telling his brother that he didn't have a daughter, remember?" Matt replied "And let's not forget that Falling Brook is a small town and rumors frequently don't have any basis in fact."

"But, hypothetically, what would happen if there is a secret love child? Will she inherit Joshua's wealth?"

"Or she could be an imposter trying to con the family out of their money," Matt suggested.

"Cynical," Emily commented.

"Very," Matt agreed. "Just like I'm cynical about your engagement to Morris."

Emily tipped her head back and released a huff of annoyance. "I was, almost, having a nice time." Emily placed her forearms on the table and lifted those big, bold eyes to meet his. They were eyes he could look into for eternity and he'd never be bored with the ever-changing shades of blue. "Can we please, please, talk about something else?"

Matt looked down at the ring on her finger and felt nausea swirl in his stomach. He so desperately wanted to rip it off her hand and toss it into the ocean.

Matt took a long sip of his beer before reluctantly nodding. "Okay. Let's not talk about jerk-face."

Wanting to go back to the easy conversation they'd been enjoying before he raised the subject of Morris—idiot!—he'd seized on the first topic to jump into his head. "We were talking about Black Crescent... I've had some discussions with Joshua Lowell about me filling the CEO position."

Surprise jumped into her eyes. "But why? I thought you were happy at MJR. And isn't MJR bigger than Black Crescent? Wouldn't that be a step down for you?"

Matt didn't hesitate to tell her his thinking behind his decision to apply for the position. "I've hit a ceiling with MJR—I've been CEO for five years and I think the shareholders have become a bit complacent about my abilities."

Emily lifted her eyebrows. "I'm trying to decide

whether you're being a boastful jerk or just ridiculously honest."

"Ridiculously honest," Matt told her, his tone sincere. "I'm very competitive and I don't like to lose."

"Is that why you are here with me?" Emily asked, and her question punched him in the gut. Until recently, he would've had to answer in the affirmative, reluctantly admitting that part of his wanting to be with her had to do with his competitive nature and his dislike for Morris.

But that had faded and Matt knew that he wanted to be with Emily, any way he could. And if all that meant was talking to her in a near-empty restaurant, he'd take it.

"I'm here because there is nowhere, right now, I'd rather be."

Emily looked doubtful and he didn't blame her; he sounded cheesy but, sometimes, the truth was cheesy. Sad but true.

Needing to get into safer water, Matt reverted back to the topic of the career. "I'm damn good at my job and I am very, very good at reading the markets. I make sure my staff keeps making MJR and our clients a lot of money. I've proved my value to the company and I'm due for a significant raise but the board is hemming and hawing."

"And you are hoping that Black Crescent will make you an offer you can take to the MJR board to force their hand."

That had been the initial plan. "But I also like the idea of taking a smaller fund and growing it as

I did for MJR. So, if Black Crescent's offer is good, I might move."

"That's not very loyal of you."

"That's unfair, Emily."

Emily frowned at his quick response. "Why? You've just told me you're happy to jump ship."

"That's business, and it's expected. But in personal relationships, and once I've decided someone is worthy of my loyalty, I'm as loyal as hell."

Matt held her eyes and slowly, softly, he saw her cynicism fade and embarrassment stroll in. "Sorry. You're right, it was an unfair comment."

Matt appreciated her apology. So many people would've moved on from the moment and brushed it off; Emily faced it head-on. "Accepted." He added, "When I make up my mind to stand in someone's corner, Em, nothing short of a bomb will dislodge me."

"And you're wanting to stand in my corner?" Emily asked, sounding dubious.

"You're catching on," Matt replied with an easy grin.

Emily nibbled on the inside of her lip, looking confused. And gorgeous. "I don't understand why because you should be running a million miles away from me. I am engaged, I've kissed you, I've basically cheated on my fiancé. On the surface, I don't seem very nice at all. Yet you are still here…*why*?"

"Apart from the fact that I can't stop imagining you in my bed, your body flushed with pleasure after I've taken you for the third time that night?"

Emily blushed at his honesty but she didn't drop

her eyes. Matt, realizing she wouldn't be distracted, took his time answering her question. "I value loyalty and, generally, I would never mess with someone who is engaged."

"But?"

"But you're different—this entire situation is different and I can't stay away from you. I want to but I can't." Matt shrugged. "You're like an itch that just won't go away."

Instead of being offended at being called an itch, Emily, thank God, just laughed. "Smooth, Velez."

Fair comment. He'd been more erudite at fourteen, for God's sake!

"I just feel like you need someone in your corner and I'm big and mean and not afraid to fight. Though it would be easier if I knew what monster we were fighting." He waggled his eyebrows in an over-the-top gesture to spill.

Emily's lips twitched and his heart rolled over in his chest. "Nice try."

"Anyway, it's far too beautiful a day to talk about your fake fiancé."

Instead of arguing, Emily just smiled. Her lack of argument piqued Matt's interest. Maybe he was finally, finally getting through to her.

Emily's tongue swirled around the head of her icecream cone and Matt stifled a groan. Thankful for the table hiding his massive erection, he tried to recall the periodic table of elements in his head but couldn't remember much beyond carbon and nitrogen.

And then all the blood in his head drained lower, much lower and he dropped ten IQ points when Emily rolled her sweet potato, maple and walnut ice cream, a specialty item on the restaurant's menu, across her tongue.

"Would you like a taste?" Emily asked, touching the corner of her mouth with the tip of her tongue. "It's delicious."

Matt squirmed in his seat, uncomfortable. "That's not what I'm desperate to taste," Matt said, his voice hoarse. "And, just to be clear, the only way I'm prepared to sample that combination of flavors would be if it is smeared over your very naked, very beautiful body."

Emily almost dropped her ice cream, her eyes widening at his frank comment. "Uh… I don't know what to say to that."

"Say yes—say that you'll let me take you to bed and put me, hopefully, us out of our misery."

Emily didn't respond as ice cream dripped off her fingers to land on the table. She didn't notice and Matt didn't care. Say yes, dammit.

"Matt…" Emily whispered.

Matt placed his forearms on the table and leaned forward, entranced by her beautiful face and her bemused expression. But under the puzzlement was desire, hot and sexy, deep, dark, royal blue flashes of encouragement. She wanted him, and the thought made Matt's chest swell.

"Come home with me, Em. Let's explore whatever is bubbling between us."

Instead of replying, Emily stood up abruptly and dropped her ice-cream cone onto the side plate on the table. She walked over to the railing and then headed for the rickety stairs leading to the beach. Matt sighed. Too much, too strong, Velez, just as always. He had no experience of treading gently; he was more of a bull in a china shop.

Emily, this situation, needed gentle handling and he'd completely blown it. Matt opened his wallet and pulled out more than enough cash to settle their bill and to provide the waitress with a big tip. He picked up Emily's bag and followed her down the stairs, realizing they ended underneath the pier. On the last step, he noticed Emily's shoes and there she was, her back against a pole, watching the waves rolling over her toes and feet.

Matt dropped her bag on top of her shoes and quickly stepped out of his flat-soled boots, whipped off his socks and tucked them into his size thirteens. He rolled up the cuffs to his pants and followed Emily's footsteps to where she stood, then stopped in front of her. The beach, like the restaurant, was deserted and it felt like they were the only two people standing on this vast Atlantic Ocean coastline.

When Emily finally lifted her eyes to look at him, she lifted her hands in the air and he saw traces of ice cream on her fingers. "I'm sticky."

Matt captured her hand and gently sucked her index finger into his mouth, tasting the sweetness of maple syrup and the earthiness of sweet potato on her skin. "That's not too bad, actually."

Emily laughed. "Now you're the one being stubborn. It was delicious, *actually*."

"Then why did you dump it and walk away?" Matt asked, placing his mouth in the center of her palm, not breaking eye contact.

"Because I didn't want to give those old men a heart attack when I did this."

Emily gripped his shirt above his heart and twisted it into her fingers to tug him forward. She stood up on her toes and touched her mouth to his, sweet and responsive and oh-so-hot.

"Make me forget, Matt. Just for a few minutes, make me forget that my life is an out-of-control wildfire," Emily whispered against his mouth.

"I can do that," Matt replied before taking her in a kiss that was as hot as the water swirling around their feet was cold. He wrapped his arms around her and yanked her close, holding the back of her head to keep her mouth on his. He nipped and suckled her lips, teasing her by not allowing his tongue to slide beyond her teeth.

Emily, surprising him, pulled her mouth off his, gripped his face in both hands, and her voice was rough when she spoke. "Seriously, Velez, kiss me like you mean it."

Well, okay then.

Matt placed his hands under her thighs and boosted her up against his body, the vee of her mound dragging over his swollen erection. He settled her there, as close as he could get her and walked her backward, carrying her under the wooden deck of the restaurant and deeper into the shadows. Placing her against another pole, he leaned into her, swirling his tongue around hers, lost in her mouth, in her sweet ice-cream-and-imp taste.

Matt anchored her against the pole as he devoured her mouth, needing more, needing everything. Knowing they were deep in the shadows of both the balcony and the pier, he placed one hand on her breast, his thumb quickly finding her swollen nipple. He ran his lips over her jaw, down her neck, sucking and nipping and relishing her breathy words of encouragement. He pulled Em's shirt from her skirt and traced his hand over her flat stomach. He yanked the material of her shirt up and then his fingers slid into the cup of her bra, pulling it aside so he could see her pretty breast, her pale pink nipple puckered and demanding to be kissed.

Bending his head, he pulled her bud into his mouth and knew that it wouldn't take much to make him blow. He hadn't been this out of control since he was sixteen and in the backseat of his first car.

Emily made him lose control and, frankly, he didn't much care. Kissing her, having her in his arms was all that important. Allowing Emily's legs to drop to the sand, he sucked her nipple onto the roof of his mouth before allowing it to pop out of his mouth, wet and glistening. He blew across its surface and Emily shuddered.

Knowing he should stop but unable to, Matt tensed when Emily's hand rested on his bulging erection, holding him through the fabric of his pants.

He should stop, he really should but she was too tempting, too responsive. He wanted her, no, he craved her. Nothing was more important than kissing and touching Emily right here and right now.

Matt pulled her skirt up her leg, allowing his hand to curl around her thigh, dangerously close to the band of her panties. He could feel her heat and when he looked into her eyes, he saw only desire there.

Then she said the magic words. "Please, Matt, touch me."

He looked around, saw that they were still alone and still concealed. It was the go-ahead he needed, the encouragement he craved. Without wasting a second, Matt took her in a searing kiss, his fingers sliding beneath the band of her lacy panties into her soft hair and down, down, down into her feminine folds. He groaned at her heat, sighed at her wet warmth on his fingers and he couldn't resist sliding his middle finger into her, his thumb finding her little bead with alacrity. Emily squealed, lifted onto her toes but Matt covered her mouth with his, not wanting to alert the patrons above as to what was happening under their feet. Not that there were any customers on the deck; he'd checked.

Matt took his kiss deeper, felt Emily respond and pushed another finger into her slick channel, knowing she was close. He wanted her to fall apart in his arms, needed this brief connection before they went back to their lives.

"Come for me, imp. But quietly," Matt told her, her lips against his mouth.

"This is madness."

Matt's lips curved into a smile. "But it's fun."

"What about you?" Emily asked, arching against his hand, trying to get closer.

"I'm good." He wasn't but there was nothing she could do about that now. Besides, only Emily and her pleasure were important; nothing else mattered. He tapped the insides of her channel with his finger and felt her body tense, moisture gushing over his fingers. Wanting her to have more, to have everything, he pressed his thumb into her clitoris and she whimpered, tensed, gushed again and gripped his biceps with strong, feminine fingers.

Then her knees buckled and Matt jerked her against him, holding her up with his free hand. He ached for release, needed it more than he needed to breathe but seeing that dazed, befuddled, satisfied-as-hell look on Emily's face made up for him not having his own happy ending.

Sort of.

Matt disengaged himself and rested his forehead against hers, his breath as ragged as hers.

"You are so incredibly beautiful."

A tiny smile touched Emily's lips and Matt watched as uneasiness strolled into her eyes and across her face. Holding her face in his hands, he forced her to look up, to meet his eyes.

"Please don't regret this." Matt saw that she was about to speak and shook his head. "This has nothing to do with…anyone else and everything to do with us."

And that was the hard truth. Right now, no one else was part of this magical moment. They were just two people who were out-of-control addicted to one another.

Emily looked like she was about to disagree but then she surprised him by nodding. She rested the back of her head against the pole and didn't object when he pulled her bra back over her breast and dropped her skirt down her thighs. Satisfied that she was tidy, he pulled her into his arms, wrapped them around her and placed his chin on top of her head.

For the first time in years he felt utterly relaxed, fully at ease. Holding her like this felt right…

And yeah, good. Holding Emily like this was, terrifyingly, something he thought he might be able to do for the rest of his life. But Matt was old enough not to pay any attention to the fuzzy feelings that rolled through one after good sex; they would fade and reality would stroll back in. Because Matt refused to allow himself to dream, need or want.

Seven

Later that evening, in her bed at home, Emily rolled over and buried her face in her pillow. She hadn't been able to forget, not for one minute, how it felt to have Matt's hand between her legs, his mouth on her nipple, her tongue in his mouth.

How he'd effortlessly brought her to her first orgasm.

Her chest tight, Emily lifted her head, sucked in some air and flipped onto her back, kicking away her bedcovers in frustration. She turned her head to look at Nico's engagement ring sitting on the bedside table, fighting the urge to toss it out the window. She should feel guilty about what happened between her and Matt on the beach but she didn't.

She wasn't in love with Nico and she had no intention of marrying him. Ever. This was a sham engagement and she owed her blackmailing fiancé no loyalty.

But she couldn't allow him to find out that Matt had touched her, with great skill, on an empty beach earlier in the day. If he did, her entire world, and her dad's and, to an extent, Davy's, would come crashing down around her. She had to tread carefully, be smart, keep her wits about her and the only way to do that was to avoid Matt Velez.

Easier said than done.

Emily still wanted him, here now. In her bed. Leaning over her, sliding into her, setting her on fire again and encouraging her to dance in the flames.

She'd had one or two boyfriends along the way, both of whom didn't last long nor knew their way around a woman's body. She'd slept with men just a handful of times and it had been awkward and bumbling and they'd walked away satisfied while she was left wondering why everyone made such a big deal about sex.

She now knew. God, how she knew. And she suspected that she'd just had a small taste of how satisfying and fulfilling lovemaking could be...

She'd love to explore this bright new world with Matt, have him introduce her to, well, *more* but that was dangerous thinking. She had, technically and in name only, a fiancé and he was threatening to destroy everything she'd worked for unless she gave him what he wanted.

But, even if Nico wasn't a factor, Matt was extremely dangerous to her emotional health. If she allowed herself to, she could love him and love never ended well for her. The people who loved her always left and Matt would not be the exception to the rule.

Emily had no intention of being left behind so she should be concentrating on how to find a way out of that mess and stop thinking about how else Matt Velez could make her scream.

Be sensible, Emily. Focus on what is important and that is saving Arnott's.

Knowing that she wouldn't be nodding off anytime soon, not with the whirling, swirling sensations sliding through her body—was this what horny felt like? How uncomfortable!—Emily left her bed, walked into her lounge and sat down behind her computer. She needed to trawl the web; if she didn't find any damaging information on Nico tonight, she would hire a PI in the morning.

Nico was making noises about wanting to marry soon and she was running out of time and choices.

Emily heard her phone chime with a message and looked at the clock on her screen; it was just past midnight. Concerned that it was Davy—she'd taken Matt's advice and given her brother some space—she hurried back into her bedroom and picked up her device, her heart lurching when she saw she had a text message from Matt.

You awake?

I am now, she typed back.

Can't stop thinking about you, what we did.

Emily tapped the front of her phone against her forehead, conscious of her heart wanting to jump out of her chest.

Em? Can I come over?

She couldn't say yes but neither could she say no. She wanted to see him but she knew that she should keep a healthy distance between them. She wanted to kiss and touch him—taking time to explore his stunning body—but she was playing with fire. The blaze she was stoking was becoming a little too big for her to handle and, if she didn't take care, it had the power to incinerate her.

And she wasn't talking about Nico finding out...

No, even if Nico wasn't a factor, Matt was dangerous. *If* this was just physical attraction, it would be easier to ignore but she *liked* Matt, she felt alive when she was in his company. She enjoyed the way he spoke and interacted with Davy, his sharp mind, the unexpected flashes of humor. She wanted to know what had put the shadows in his eyes, what forces had shaped him into being the man he was today.

She liked his broad hands and his slow smile, his dark hair and intense eyes. The way he spoke and, God, she adored the way he made her feel.

She liked him, she always had, and Em knew that if she allowed it too, that like could turn into something deeper. Something hazardous.

Love, as she knew, was dangerous; it was unpredictable and selfish and transactional. And, worst of all, it had no staying power. Love wasn't something she trusted.

So no, she would not allow herself to fall in love with any man. She didn't need affection, she just wanted to be free of Nico and for her family's reputation to remain unblemished.

That wasn't so much to ask, was it?

Fifteen minutes later, Emily heard the brisk rap and, with a wildly beating heart, opened the door to see Matt holding the top frame of it, his face reflecting the frustration she knew he was feeling.

"I'm not sleeping with you," she told him, not bothering with a standard greeting. Was she trying to convince herself or him? Did it matter?

All she knew was that if Matt made love to her, properly, she might slide deeper into like and be halfway to love. Not happening.

"Can I come in?" Matt asked, dropping those sexy arms with their big biceps and raised veins.

Emily nodded and stepped back, gesturing him inside. She didn't put on a light and they looked at each other in the moonlight, a million unsaid thoughts arcing between them.

"I won't sleep with you."

"I heard you, imp," Matt said, sounding weary. He scrubbed his hands over his face. "I just needed to see that you were okay. You were pretty quiet on the trip back to town."

That was because she was still riding a sexual high

and an emotional roller coaster. "I'm fine," Em replied. She gestured to the door. "If that's all, then you can go."

"Dammit, stop trying to push me away!" Matt snapped.

"I have to! I can't do this!" Emily shouted, her frustration bubbling over.

"Why? Because you're engaged to that prick? If you love him, there is no way you would've let me do what I did to you!" Matt returned her shout but not for one second did his anger frighten her. Emily knew that Matt would never ever hurt her. Not physically anyway.

"I never said I loved him," Emily quietly replied, dropping to the edge of the nearest chair.

Matt dropped to his haunches in front of her and placed his hands on her knees. "Then why the hell are you marrying him? Explain that to me."

She wished she could. Emily could only put her elbows on her knees and bury her face in her hands.

Matt's hand landed on her head, his touch as soft as a butterfly. "I wish you'd let me help you, sweetheart."

"This is something I need to do on my own, Matteo."

"I suspect that you've been on your own for too long," Matt disagreed. "But I'm not going to argue with you about that now. You're exhausted and you need to sleep."

Em dropped her hands before managing a tired shrug. "I can't sleep. I haven't been able to sleep for more than a few hours recently."

"I bet your sleep problems coincided with His Awfulness putting that ugly rock on your finger," Matt muttered as he stood up. In one smooth movement, he slid an arm around her back and another under her thighs and lifted her against his chest.

"What the hell! Put me down."

Matt's mouth touched her temple. "Relax, imp," Matt ordered as he carried her across the room, down the hallway and into her bedroom. He carefully placed her on the bed and pulled the covers up to her waist. Emily watched, mouth agape, as he shed his clothing, his beautiful body lithe and muscled. God, he was lovely, she thought. Wide shoulders, a perfect amount of hair on his muscled chest, that rippled stomach.

And a very nice package under a tight pair of black boxer briefs.

She watched him swell under her scrutiny and she lifted her hands. "We're not making love and you need to go!"

"We're not making love but I'm staying," Matt calmly replied. He pulled back the covers, slid into bed next to her and hauled her onto his chest. He placed one hand low on her butt and gave her a reassuring pat. "The Asshat is still in Chicago so you can relax."

Matt kissed her temple, much like he did earlier, and held his lips there. "Let me hold you while you sleep, imp."

"I can't do this. I'm better off being alone." But he was so warm and with her cheek on his shoulder, she felt so comfortable and safe. In his embrace, Emily felt like nothing could hurt her and that, one day, everything would be okay.

"No, you only think you are better off," Matt replied, his voice a deep rumble. "But let's argue about that later—for now, just let me hold you while you sleep."

Emily didn't have the energy to argue; she felt her eyes closing and she snuggled closer, her thigh coming up to rest on Matt's, her knee brushing the underside of his briefs. This was so lovely, but she couldn't get used to it. This was only one night but it would be a memory she'd hold on to for the rest of her life.

"Em?"

"Mmm?" She was so close to fading away, in that delicious state on the edge of unconsciousness.

"Promise me that you'll come to me if you start considering doing something dangerous, illegal, stupid or consequential. If you ever get scared and don't know who else to turn to, turn to me."

"Mmm, promise."

And then there was just warmth and safety and the blessed relief of sleep.

Work the next day was a disaster and Matt, knowing when to quit, leaned back in his chair and glared at the complicated and detailed spreadsheet on his screen.

He'd made a mistake on a formula and couldn't figure out where he went wrong.

He knew that frustration was part of the deal when

you ran a massive company but making mistakes because he couldn't concentrate was unacceptable. Not being able to concentrate because his brain kept returning to yesterday and time spent with Emily frustrated the hell out of him. He never allowed a woman to distract him...

It wasn't who he was or what he did.

Crap.

Maybe he was tired. Or horny. Or both. He hadn't slept much last night and he wanted, no, he needed sex.

Desperately. Immediately.

Matt ran a hand through his hair, knowing that he could take care of the immediate problem himself but it simply wasn't the same. He didn't want to do it solo, hell, neither did he want to find a willing partner for a little fun.

No, because life was screwing with him, he only wanted Emily.

She was the satisfaction he needed.

He was ass deep in trouble.

Matt linked his fingers behind his neck and looked across the room when his door opened. Vee, wearing a dress the color of cold custard marched into the room and stopped on the other side of his desk, hands on her hips.

"What have I done now?" Matt asked, instantly wary.

"Joshua Lowell has been trying to reach you on your cell but he says it keeps going to voice mail." Vee reached across his desk and picked up his phone, frowning at the blank screen. "Is it turned off or is the battery dead?"

"Battery." He'd taken the phone with him to Em's and it died sometime during the night. He'd left her place shortly before dawn to make the trip into the city and charging his phone had been way down on his list of priorities. "Did Joshua leave a message?"

Annoyance flashed in Vee's eyes. "He wants to see you, if it suits you, at Black Crescent at four p.m."

Matt picked up his pen and tapped the end on his desk. "Did he say why?"

"A follow-up meeting to the one you had," Vee replied. "He was being coy but, reading between the lines, I presume he has more questions." Vee shook her head. "I'm not sure if working at Black Crescent is going to suit me, Matteo."

Matt sucked down his laughter. "I'll bear that in mind."

Vee nodded before narrowing her eyes at him. "You're very distracted at the moment. It's unlike you."

She had no idea. He was crazy in lust with an angelic blonde who was anything but angelic and was as stubborn as hell. A woman who made him act in ways he never had before. He didn't do sleepovers—they tended to give his sexual partners ideas he didn't need them to entertain—but last night he'd held a woman in his arms without the payoff of sex. And, worst of all, he'd liked it.

He liked her smell, the way she fit in his arms, her

soft snuffle-snore, the way strands of her white-blond hair caught in his stubble.

Man, he was fast losing it. And he had to get it together, sooner rather than later.

Yes, he liked Emily and yes, he was fiercely attracted to her. No, he wasn't falling in love with her. He just wanted to help her because something was hinky with her engagement to Falling Brook's resident ass.

Every day his feelings for Emily became a little more intense and a great deal more complicated. Initially, he'd pursued her because of their hectic attraction and because of his competitive nature. Morris, his old rival, had someone he'd always wanted and he'd been envious and pissed that he'd succeeded where Matt'd failed.

But, recently—and finally—pride and ego had taken a backseat. Something was bubbling between him and Emily and he had to get a handle on it before it spilled over and scalded them both. If he wasn't careful, he'd resurrect those old dreams and wants— her in his bed, the mother of his children, his forever lover—and that was unacceptable.

Whatever they had would end at some point so maybe he should just listen to Emily and allow her the space to work through whatever was happening between her and Sir Scumbag.

So maybe he should give her a little time, trust her to handle Nico in her own way.

Emily had promised him that she'd come to him

if she found herself in more trouble than she could handle and he could live with that.

For now.

After receiving another message from Joshua asking him to delay their meeting until after five thirty, Matt arrived at Black Crescent and stood in the waiting area outside Joshua's office. Before leaving for the day, Joshua's assistant Haley told him that Joshua was just finishing a call and would be with him in a few minutes.

Matt, not in a hurry and not having anywhere to go—and ignoring the fact that he desperately wanted to see Emily's lovely face—leaned his shoulder into the glass pane and stared down onto the wooded area behind Black Crescent's building. Emily's house was a few miles down this same road and her bedroom window had the same view of the same woods, deep and dark and mysterious.

Emily…man, he had to stop thinking about her.

Matt heard footsteps behind him and turned his head to see a younger version of Joshua Lowell striding across the room. It had been years since he'd seen Oliver Lowell but Matt recognized him instantly because his resemblance to Joshua was so strong.

Without breaking his stride, Oliver jerked his chin in a silent greeting and walked into Joshua's office without knocking. Matt glared at his disappearing back; he had an appointment with Joshua and he didn't like to be kept waiting. Oliver slammed the office door behind him but the lock didn't latch and the door eased back open.

"Are you meeting with Matt Velez to discuss the CEO position?"

"I am."

Matt debated whether to tell the Lowell brothers that the room had excellent acoustics and he could hear every word they said, or if he should walk across the room and close the door.

"Look, I understand why you are looking outside the family for a CEO," Oliver said. "I don't have the best track record."

No, Matt thought, he didn't. For most of his twenties, Oliver, so he heard, had a fondness for cocaine, but he was, apparently, clean now and had been for many years. But people had long memories and Oliver might not be the best choice to head up a company with an already tarnished reputation.

"Matt's been waiting on me for at least ten minutes, Ol. I need to talk to him," Joshua said, sounding impatient.

"I know but I really need to talk to you. It's important."

Matt heard a strange note in Oliver's voice and frowned. The guy sounded angry but under the anger he heard panic and confusion. He obviously needed to talk to Joshua and Oliver was lucky to have a big brother to turn to. Matt's big brother had never had the time, or the inclination, or been encouraged by their parents, to look after his younger sibling.

When he got scared and worried or panicked, he

had to suck it up and deal because his brother always and forever came first.

Matt made a decision, walked over to the door and rapped on the frame. After pushing the door open, he looked across the large office to a frustrated looking Joshua Lowell.

"You guys talk—we can do this another time," Matt said.

Joshua shook his head and waved Matt inside. "No, you were good enough to come down so take a seat, Matt." Joshua pointed a finger at Oliver. "My brother Oliver. Ol, this is Matt Velez."

Oliver stood up to shake hands with Matt and after Joshua invited him to sit down, the older brother turned to Oliver. "Sit, stay, be quiet."

Oliver rolled his eyes. "Once a younger brother, always a younger brother."

Matt smiled at him, liking him. He might have once been the Lowell family screwup, but it seemed like he'd turned his life around. Good for him.

Joshua cleared his throat and Matt turned his attention back to the man he most needed to impress.

He and Joshua ran through most of the same questions he'd been asked before and Matt stifled his impatience; they were rehashing old ground. Matt felt like Joshua was looking for a chink in his armor and Matt, feeling antsy, cut to the chase. "Come on, Joshua, what's this all about? We've covered this ground in our previous meetings. I can do this job and I can do it well. You know it, I know it, so what's the problem?"

"Straight to the point," Oliver murmured. "I like that."

Matt and Joshua, engaged in a silent battle of wills, both ignored him. Joshua eventually broke the silence by picking up a very expensive pen and twisting it through his fingers. "You say all the right things, Matt, and your résumé is as impressive as hell."

Matt didn't react. "But?"

"But a part of me is wondering how serious you are at jumping ship," Joshua stated. "This company needs a hundred and ten percent commitment, that's why I'm stepping down, but you haven't given our discussion all your attention."

Matt internally winced. Okay, Joshua was seriously astute because once or twice, or ten or fifteen times, his thoughts had drifted to Emily, remembering the way she fell apart in his arms on the beach, the curves of her body, what trouble she was in with Morris.

He never allowed himself to be distracted, to focus on anything other than business...

Especially when he was conducting business.

Matt swallowed his heavy sigh. Up until Emily dropped back into his life, his personal life never bled into his business world.

"I apologize if you think I've haven't been attentive," Matt said smoothly, not admitting the truth. "But if it's any reassurance, I have an incredible ability to multitask. I just don't have a lot of patience for waiting around."

Joshua's expression remained unreadable but Matt

saw the amusement in his eyes. Thinking he'd leave while he was ahead, Matt stood up and leaned across the table to shake Joshua's hand. "Do what's best for Black Crescent. And no hard feelings if you choose to go for another candidate." He slid a look at Oliver. "You two need to talk so I'll leave you to it."

Oliver stood up, shook Matt's hand and met his gaze straight on. No blinking, no embarrassment. This guy had fought his demons, conquered his drug addiction and it was obvious that he was trying to win at life.

Good for him. That deserved his respect.

Eight

Nico was back from his conference in Chicago and, on getting his imperious text message telling her to meet him at L'Albri at seven on the dot, Emily felt sharp-bladed knives tap dancing in her stomach.

Emily parked her car, pulled her coat over her cocktail dress and avoided a puddle on her way to the restaurant. Standing outside the brightly lit windows, she peered inside and saw Nico sitting at the bar talking to two men she didn't recognize.

She couldn't keep up the charade; she wanted out...

Tonight, immediately.

But her choices were limited. If she handed Nico his ring back, he'd release those photographs and his false documents and the Arnott name and reputation would be ruined.

Along with the loss of their credibility, the loss of their income would mean forfeiting their house and their savings would be soon wiped out...

So, no, allowing Nico to besmirch the company was not an option.

Her only option was to blackmail Nico back but she'd yet to discover anything about him that was greater or equal to his fake information on Arnott's. She'd yet to find any dirt on her fake fiancé and the PI she'd hired hadn't found anything either. Sure, Nico wasn't a model citizen: he'd had a few dodgy girlfriends—not unexpected—and a couple of business deals that were sleazy but not illegal. She had nothing she could hold over him.

She didn't have nearly enough to make him go away.

Maybe if she got her hands on his phone or on his computer, she'd find something she could use, but Nico guarded those devices like the Secret Service guarded the president's nuclear codes.

But she had one more option... Maybe she could tell Matt about his blackmailing scheme; maybe he knew something or could think of a way to help her. He and Nico had worked together years ago; maybe he could point her in the right direction. Matt wasn't an angel, he was a hard, tough businessman and he had a reputation for thinking outside the box. And he seemed to like her...

Emily thought back to how right it felt to fall asleep

in his arms, to feel his smile on her skin, to look into those intense brown eyes. She enjoyed Matt's company and she liked him more than she should.

And if her life was anything near normal, and if she believed in love, she could easily see herself falling for him. He was smart, successful, sexy. Oh, he was also impatient and demanding and occasionally bossy, but under his alphaness was a guy with a tender heart. He was a protector but could she trust him?

She thought that maybe, just maybe, she could.

But she couldn't afford to be impulsive and she needed to give the idea of talking to Matt, asking for his help, a little thought. She couldn't take days to come to a decision, she didn't have that much time to waste, but she could take a few hours, a day or two. Emily saw Nico looking at his watch, the frown pulling his brows together, and knew that she needed to go inside, to act like the happy fiancée, to simper and smile and act excited about her upcoming wedding.

Frankly, she'd rather roll around in honey and lie on an anthill.

Emily pushed open the door to the bar, shrugged off her coat and draped it over her arm. Walking into the bar area, she managed to pull a smile on to her face as she strolled up to Nico.

"Welcome back," Emily said as he remained seated on his barstool, leaving her to stand next to him, still holding her coat and bag. "How was your conference?"

"Interesting," Nico replied. He picked up his whiskey and sipped from the rim, giving her a long up-

and-down look. Dressed in a plain black, simple but classic cocktail dress, she knew that he couldn't find fault with what she was wearing. She'd pulled her hair back into a sleek ponytail, her makeup was understated and she was sure she didn't have lipstick on her teeth.

She desperately wanted to be with a man who thought she was gorgeous dressed in a baggy T-shirt, leggings and with smudged mascara. She wanted a man who made her feel like she was his world and not a means to padding his bank account…

She wanted Matt.

As what? Her lover? Partner? Husband?

Number one was, maybe, possible but option two and three? Those weren't viable. Matt wasn't the type to settle down and she didn't believe in love anyway. It was too vague, too restless an emotion.

Love was simply too risky.

Pulling her attention off Matt and what could never be, Emily smiled at the men Nico was talking to, introducing herself because Nico hadn't. She engaged in the usual getting-to-know-you chitchat and accepted an offer for a glass of white wine from the gentleman to his left.

Emily, ignoring Nico's brooding gaze, sipped her wine, furious that Nico hadn't offered her a seat, introduced her or ordered her a drink.

If this was any other man she'd be walking out the door…

Emily felt the energy in the room change and she turned around, immediately noticing Matt's tall, broad frame walking toward her, carrying a barstool in one hand. When he reached her, he placed the stool next to her and offered her his hand to help her up onto the seat. When she was seated, Matt took her bag, hung it over the back of her chair and plucked her coat from her hands.

"I'll ask one of the waitresses to hang it up," he told Emily, his words accompanied by a blistering look at Nico's now furious face.

"Hey, stop fussing over my fiancée," Nico complained. His words sounded slurred and Emily's heart sank. Yay, Nico was already drunk. This was going to be a lovely evening. Not.

"I'm just treating her with some basic respect," Matt whipped back. "You should try it sometime."

Emily caught Matt's angry eyes and shook her head, silently begging him not to antagonize Nico. There was too much at stake.

Matt narrowed his eyes at her and when he turned to their companions and introduced himself, Emily frowned. Oh God, he wasn't planning on joining them, was he? She couldn't juggle her half-drunk fiancé and her sexy lover. She wasn't that sophisticated.

"Are you really engaged to Nico?"

Emily jerked her head up at the incredulous question from the man to her right and nodded. She lifted up her left hand and wiggled her fingers, ignoring Matt's blistering scowl. "I am."

"Huh. That's quite a rock."

It was ugly and she hated it. "Thank you." What else could she say?

The other man, standing next to Matt—who'd yet to walk away, damn him!—picked up her hand to examine her ring. "Congratulations, I hope you'll be very happy." Was she imagining the doubt in his voice?

Emily tugged her fingers out of his grip, ignoring Matt's sardonic look. She needed to change the subject, and quickly, but before she could, the man next to her lobbed another question into the awkward silence.

"She's too angelic looking for you, Morris. Are you blackmailing her to marry you?" His blithe question was accompanied by a loud guffaw and a slap on Nico's back.

The words plowed through Emily, with all the force of a .45 Magnum.

Do not react, do not react, do not...

She felt the world whirling, then swirling, and then black dots appeared in front of her eyes. Then, from a place far, far away, she felt Matt's hand on her back, his touch light but reassuring. Within a few seconds it was gone, but the sensation of falling left her and she could breathe.

Laugh, say something, brush it off but do it now. Right now.

"You have a very overactive imagination." Emily made herself look at Nico. Icy fingers walked up her spine as she saw the hot fury in his eyes. "Shall we head into the dining room? I'm absolutely starving."

Emily was being blackmailed.

Matt couldn't believe that he hadn't considered the

possibility before this but, while he knew that Nico was a grade-A bastard, he had never considered he'd sink so low.

But Matt had seen her reaction to that casual, jokey question and while he didn't think anyone else had caught the terror in her eyes, her stiff body and her shaky breath, he had. She'd brushed off the suggestion as being ludicrous and everybody bought her wide-eyed explanation.

Except for him.

Because while she hid her distress well, he'd spent enough time with his imp to know when she was acting her ass off. And her performance tonight would've earned a goddamn Oscar.

Matt stood in the shadowed area below the stairs leading to her apartment and prayed Morris wouldn't accompany Emily home. If he did, he might be facing assault charges in the morning because there was no way he'd be able to keep his hands from rearranging that supercilious face.

Matt needed to know what dirt Morris had on Emily. There was no way he was going to allow her to be blackmailed into marriage with that scumbag.

Matt heard the rumble of a car and, thankful for the distraction from his thoughts, slid deeper into the shadows. He relaxed fractionally when he saw it was Emily's car making its way up the driveway and he waited to see who exited the car she parked in her space in the four-car garage.

He exhaled when he saw that she was alone. Matt watched as she approached him, taking in her pale face and haunted eyes. He was about to step into the light but hesitated, knowing that him jumping out of the shadows would scare her. His gut screamed for him to stay hidden and when another car sped up the driveway, he sent a prayer heavenward that he'd parked his car down the road and he stayed where he was.

Emily turned slowly and watched as Morris stopped his car next to her. He was half-plowed at the restaurant and he was driving? What an asshat.

Emily, Matt noticed, didn't move when his passenger window slid down.

"What are you doing here, Nico?" Emily demanded, her voice full of loathing. "We didn't exactly leave the restaurant on good terms."

"I'm happy with the outcome."

"Because you're holding all the cards."

"Yes, I am," Morris replied, his voice cold. "Let me come up—we can open up a glass of wine, forget about tonight's unpleasantness and start fresh."

Emily took a moment to reply but when she did, her words were coated with venom. "Are you kidding me? After the way you acted tonight? I'd rather have a glass of wine with a three-foot slug!"

Matt couldn't see the expression on Morris's face but he could feel the tension crackling between them. If Nico stepped out of the car and forced his way into Em's apartment, he'd rip his face off.

But Nico, luckily, leaned back in his seat and released a low chuckle. "At some point you are going to realize that my way is the only way, Emily."

Emily rubbed her forehead with the tips of her fingers and, in the shadows, Matt could see the fatigue and frustration on her face. For that alone, he could beat Morris to a pulp. "Just go, Nico."

"Since you are being so unreasonable, I think that's a good idea," Morris replied, his voice soft and menacing. "And I hope, by morning, your attitude will be adjusted."

Without replying, Emily turned to walk up her stairs. Matt held his breath but she didn't notice him standing below her, his dark clothes blending into the shadows.

Morris shut off his engine, opened his car door, stood up and, like an animal sensing danger, sniffed the air. Matt felt his heart rate speed up, its beat so loud he was convinced Morris could hear it.

Emily might have the survival instincts of a blind gazelle on the African plains but Morris wasn't a fool.

Matt considered his options: he could walk out now and confront him, and the urge to do exactly that was strong. But, if he remained hidden, he could find another way to attack later…and it would hurt for longer.

But if Nico found him hiding in the shadows, all bets were off. Matt didn't move, didn't breathe for ten, twenty, thirty seconds? It felt like a century.

For the rest of his life, Matt would be grateful that Morris climbed back into his car, started the engine and drove away.

Matt waited for five minutes, then another five just in case Morris decided his first instinct was right.

And when his gut stopped screaming at him, he took the stairs to Emily's apartment three at a time. And when he hit the landing, he lifted his hand to tap the door to find it opened to his touch.

When he stepped into the room, Emily's soft voice drifted over to him. "It took you long enough to get your ass up here, Velez."

She'd known he was there, standing under the stairs. She'd felt his presence as soon as she'd left her car but her inner voice had screamed at her not to acknowledge his nearness, to pretend she hadn't noticed him.

And thank God she'd listened because a few minutes later, Nico, doing his disgusting stalker thing, had roared up the drive to check on her. She'd been terrified he'd leave his vehicle and force his way inside but, thank the Lord and all his angels, he'd decided against following her up the stairs.

If he hadn't, Matt might be facing assault charges around about now.

Emily stared at him standing by her doorway, looking hard and tough and a little bewildered. She fought the urge to switch on a lamp because she knew that would show two silhouettes instead of one, so she left the light off and waited for her eyes to adjust. His black Henley clung to his muscles and hard body like a second skin.

His hair was messy and his eyes glowed with anger and fear and frustration.

"Emily, what the hell is going on?"

Emily wanted to lay all her troubles at his feet, to beg him to help her but she couldn't do that. This was her problem and he wasn't her Sir Galahad. That wasn't a role he had any interest in playing…

She would not throw herself at his feet, let him rescue her. She'd vowed to be self-reliant and she didn't want to renege on that promise to herself.

But damn, she was tempted. The situation between her and Nico was escalating and she had to tread softly, carefully. After tonight, she couldn't take any more chances with Matt; Nico was more dangerous than she thought and she couldn't risk Arnott's over her temporary infatuation for Matt.

She needed to force Matt out of her life, make him leave, make sure that he had no interest in coming back. And she'd do that but first she wanted one night with him. She wanted to have the memories of one explosive, thrilling night to carry her through whatever came next.

She was out of options but she could have one night.

Emily walked over to Matt and, after nudging Fatty aside with her foot—her cat seemed as enamored with Matt as she was—placed her hands on his hips and rested her forehead on his chest. "I know that you have a million questions and I can't answer any of them."

"Let me help you, imp," Matt begged, his lips in her hair. "He's blackmailing you, isn't he?"

Her shoulders sank. "Let's not do this now, okay?"

Emily tugged Matt's Henley up his chest to find

his warm, hard-with-muscle skin. "Let's do something else right now."

Matt pulled back to stare down at her, doubt in his eyes. "Are you sure? You've got a lot on your mind…"

"I need this, Matt. I need *you*."

Matt lifted his hands; the pads of his fingers skimmed her lips, her cheekbones, the sweep of her jaw. His gentle touch surprised her; it wasn't something she'd expected and it was exactly what she needed. A little gentleness, some tenderness.

Matt knew what she needed and she sank against him, reveling in the knowledge that a tough man could be so tender.

Matt cradled her head in both hands and his thumbs drifted over her eyebrows, down her temples and across her cheekbones. She didn't want to rush this and while she wanted more, she somehow knew that dragging out their release would make this first night—their only night—so much more special. Emily wanted his mouth, his lips on hers, and finally, after many minutes, far too many minutes, Matt lowered his head and his mouth skimmed hers, once, twice, before his mouth fastened on hers. Emily tried to pull him closer, to force him to give her more but he kept the tempo slow, leisurely feeding her kisses.

Heat rushed through her but, strangely, she felt shivery, like she was running a fever. Em looked into his dark eyes, hot and frothing with desire, and swallowed.

Chemistry was such a tame word to describe what was fizzing between them. Matt drove her crazy, in the best way possible. She'd wanted him years ago but that tame want didn't compare to how much she craved him now. Their attraction was bigger and bolder and brighter and Em thought there was a possibility they'd set the room alight.

It was a chance she was willing to take.

They kissed, slow, long, drugging exchanges of discovery, and Em touched him wherever she could. She slid her hand up and under his shirt, exploring his back, the bumps of his spine, the curve of his ass. Needing to know every inch of him, she brushed her fingers down his sides, allowed her tips to dance across the ridges of his stomach. He was so male, intensely, indescribably, powerfully masculine. Emily traced the long length of his sexy hip muscles and ran her finger under the band of his pants, feeling strong and utterly feminine.

Needing him a little out of control, Emily stroked his erection, from base to tip and was rewarded by a low curse and garbled laugh. She undid the first button to his jeans, then popped open the ones below.

"Not playing fair, Arnott."

Emily looked up at him. "I'm not playing at all, Velez."

After she slipped her hand inside his briefs, pushed down the material and freed him, Matt turned her and placed her hands against the wall. This was what she wanted, something new, something delicious, something out of her comfort zone. Trusting Matt, she allowed him to drag her zip down, spread open the panels of her dress, and she sighed when he placed his open mouth on each bump of her spine. She felt the clasp of her bra opening and watched as her dress and the lace-covered cups dropped to the floor below her feet. His hands traced her ribs, drifted across her stomach and then he cupped her breasts in his hands, groaning as he buried his face in her neck, sucking on that spot where her neck and shoulder met.

"I want you," he muttered. "I've wanted you from the moment I first saw you."

Emily groaned as he teased her nipples, hitting an exquisite point between arousal, need and pain. "I want your lips on me. I need you to kiss me," she murmured, her voice raspy with need.

Matt spun her around and his eyes drilled into hers. "Where?"

Emily felt flattened by the desire she saw in his eyes, desire for her. It was heady, potent and made her feel like she was all woman and all powerful. "Everywhere, Matt."

Matt smiled, then bent his knees and pulled her nipple into his mouth, his tongue swirling over her nub. Emily felt the corresponding rush of heat between her legs and groaned aloud.

"Matt, I—aah, that feels so amazing," she muttered as Matt swapped his attention to her other breast.

"And we haven't even gotten to the good part yet."

Matt, impatient now, quickly kicked away her clothes and Emily was surprised at her lack of inhibition. But how could she feel shy when Matt was looking at her like she hung the stars and moon, like he was convinced that making love to her was all that was on his mind?

Matt dropped to his knees and rested his forehead on her stomach, his hands digging into her hips. He hooked his thumbs into her lacy panties and pulled down her thong. He stared at her thin strip of hair and she gasped as he ran his finger over its softness "I can't wait to taste you. You're so hot."

Emily widened her legs and her eyes rolled back in her head when he kissed her hip bone, then the inside of her leg, his cheek brushing, ever so gently, over her mound.

Tiny flashes of bright, hot lights danced behind her eyes. "Matteo…"

"My beautiful imp," Matt murmured and finally slipped his finger between her folds and touched her…there, right there. Emily shook as a combination of emotion and sensation rushed through her system, sensitizing every inch of her skin. She could barely think, breathe and then his hot, clever finger slipped inside her, followed by another. His thumb swept over her clit and Emily felt the pressure building.

"I'm so close," she whispered, all her focus on what he was doing to her.

"Not yet," Matt told her, leaning back to look up at her, his fingers still deeply embedded in her.

"I can't wait."

"You can, you must." Matt's voice, rough and sexy, flowed across her skin. Not hesitating, he leaned forward to kiss her, curling his tongue around her sensitive bud. He sucked her, once and then again, and his fingers pumped into her and Emily felt herself falling and flying, both at the same time.

Would he catch her or would he let her fall? It didn't matter; all that mattered was the ride, a unique combination of joy, pleasure, a sexy high. It was everything she'd heard and read about but better. Em didn't want the feeling to end.

She didn't want anything to do with Matt to end… he was the only man she could imagine doing this to her, in this and in a million different ways, until the end of her life. He was what she needed, in a lover and in a man.

When the lights behind her eyelids dimmed and lost their color and the mini-earthquakes deep inside her stopped, Matt pulled his fingers from between her thighs and held her hips, tipping his head to look up at her.

Matt stood up in a graceful fluid movement and held out his hand. "I want you, Em. I want tonight. Come to bed with me?"

Saying no simply wasn't an option.

Nine

Emily woke up slowly and turned her head to see the soft fingers of dawn sliding through the night sky. She patted the bed and found it empty and, rolling onto her back, she placed her arm over her eyes and released a couple of creative curses. Matt was gone and she was alone.

She'd heard that guys tended to withdraw after sex but she'd hadn't expected Matt to leave without a goodbye or even a thanks for a good time. Emily furiously blinked away hot tears, angry that she was even allowing herself to feel emotional.

What did she expect? That Matt, fully aware that she was engaged to another man, would pull her into his arms and promise her the moon and stars and to purchase her a pet unicorn? No, she and Matt had been building up to this night; they'd been playing with fire since their first kiss and last night they'd stepped into the flames.

They'd stoked the fire, built it up to a bonfire and tossed on some gas. But morning was here and the coals were dying, as all good fires tended to do.

"Morris is blackmailing you. With what?"

Emily shot up at his deep voice and whipped her head around to see Matt sitting in the chair in the corner, fully dressed and his expression serious. Emily sat up and, noticing she was still naked, pulled the covers up and tucked them under her arms. Needing a minute to wrap her head around the notion that Matt was still here, that he'd been watching her sleep, she pushed her hair off her face and looked out the window. The sky was turning from black to gray and he needed to go…

"Matt, you can't be here. I can't afford for anyone to know what we…" she gestured to the bed next to her, "did."

"I'm not going anywhere until we thrash this out." Matt moved from the chair and sat on the side of her bed, hoisting his thigh up onto the mattress. "We've been dancing around the subject for weeks now and last night you pretty well confirmed he was blackmailing you. Let me help you!"

Emily stared at him, so tempted to take the hand he held out and to let him in. Could she trust him? Then she remembered the blistering words Nico tossed at her last night and she shook her head. "I can't. Last night he told me to stay away from you and if I didn't, that there would be consequences, for you. I can't risk your career and reputation."

Matt snorted, not looking the least bit worried. He placed his big hand on her thigh. "I'm a big boy and I can take care of myself."

Emily saw the confidence in his eyes and the self-belief and one of the many knots in her stomach loosened. But he needed to know what he was risking. "He threatened to report you to the Securities and Exchange Commission if I didn't break off all contact with you."

Matt's dark eyebrows inched upward. "He can try but since all the trades I oversee are completely ethical and aboveboard, he can shove his complaint up his ass."

Another knot loosened at Matt's complete dismissal of Nico's threat. "Are you sure? He could make trouble for you."

Matt put his hand on the mattress behind him and leaned back. "I run a well-known and well-respected company, the company Morris left under a bit of a cloud. I'm not in the least afraid of what he'll do or say because there's nothing there."

Emily looked at him and he frowned at the doubt he saw on her face. "You don't believe me?" he asked.

Emily pushed her hand through her messy hair. "Of course I do, it's just that Nico has resources and he's not afraid to put a false spin on a situation."

"Is that what he's done to you?" Matt gently asked her.

Emily asked Matt to pass her dressing gown from

the back of the chair next to her bed. After slipping into the gown, she slowly knotted the cord, sat down on the bed and faced him.

"Why is talking to me so hard for you, sweetheart?"

Emily took her time answering him. "A couple of years ago I promised myself that I would never rely on anyone ever again, that I would be independent and utterly self-reliant."

"We'll get back to Morris and his blackmail attempt in a minute, but why would you do that?" Matt asked. "Why is being self-reliant so important to you?"

This was like slowly picking the scab off a festering wound. "Because I got tired of people letting me down, of looking for the good opinion and validation of others. Because relying on people gives them importance in your life and everybody I've ever thought to be important has left me, in one way or another. My mom, my dad…"

Matt tipped his head to the side. "Your dad is, I presume, sleeping in his bed in that big house across the driveway."

Emily pulled a face. "Physically maybe, but he left me emotionally the time my mom did."

"Ah."

Emily stood and walked over to her window, looking out to the still-dark forest. "I guess that's a perfect segue into me telling you about Nico…"

After gathering her thoughts, Emily spoke again. "After my mom left, my dad sank into a deep depres-

sion. When he came out of it, he threw himself into
building up Arnott's into a boutique wealth-management
firm and recovering what he lost in the Black Crescent
scandal. Dad became a semi-recluse and workaholic
and one of the reasons I took the job at Arnott's was
because I thought it was the only way I'd ever see him."

Emily felt Matt's presence behind her but, instead
of touching her, he moved in front of her and mirrored
her stance, shoulder pressed into the glass window.

"Go on, imp."

Emily ran her tongue over her teeth. "Because of
Davy, Dad found a niche market looking after the financial interests of vulnerable, wealthy adults who
are incapable of managing their own affairs. A lot of
their income is tied up in trusts, sometimes not, and
Dad, through Arnott's, is their financial adviser. We
also pay the bills and report to the trusts or guard-
ians on a monthly basis. Our reputation for honesty
and integrity and playing by the rules is sacrosanct."

"You're dealing with other people's money but,
because your clients are designated as vulnerable,
it's even more important to be blemish-free," Matt
stated, quickly connecting the dots.

Emily nodded, feeling miserable.

"And, correct me if I'm wrong, Nico has something
on you that will tarnish that reputation."

Emily nodded again.

"What does he have on you?"

If she told him, there was no going back. It was
like she was on the surgeon's table, wide-eyed and

awake, about to be sliced open and not knowing if it would hurt or not.

"Em…"

"He has a picture of my dad shaking hands with the head of the Russian mob on the East Coast." Emily rushed her words, as if saying them quickly would make them less horrible.

Matt frowned. "Say again? Your dad is friends with a mobster?"

Emily was gratified to hear the disbelief in his voice. She waved his words away, agitated. "My dad doesn't have friends, not really. But he does visit Davy at Brook Village and he struck up a conversation with another father, Ivan Sokolov, who we know as John. Nico took a photo of them and he's threatened to start a rumor saying that Arnott's is laundering money for the mob and that Dad uses the residential home as cover for his meetings with John."

"Holy crap."

Emily jammed her hands into the pockets of her gown. "Being associated with the mob will destroy our reputation, Matt. We can't have our clients harboring even a whiff of suspicion about our integrity."

Matt rubbed his thumb over her cheekbone. "I understand that, but a photograph detailing one meeting? Are you not giving it too much power, especially since you say it was just that one time?"

"I can't take that chance," Emily said, placing her hand on his chest. Just touching him made her feel stronger, more anchored. And God, yes, she felt like Matt had lifted a boulder off her chest.

Matt covered her hand with his and squeezed. "And why haven't you told your dad any of this?"

Emily shrugged and dropped her eyes, then stared at the floor. She felt Matt lift her chin and she took a long time meeting his eyes. When she did, she saw sympathy but also a healthy dose of determination. He wasn't going to let her off the hook.

He was going to make her admit her worst fear, the one she'd never fully been able to think. Every time the thought started to form, she pushed it away, not prepared to deal with it.

"Why not, sweetheart?"

Emily's eyes burned with unshed tears. "I didn't tell him because—"

She released a tiny sob and shook her head.

Matt pulled her against his chest, his big arms enveloping and protecting her. "Because you couldn't trust him to stand in the ring with you? Because you couldn't trust him to put your happiness before the company reputation? Because you were afraid he would insist that you marry Morris?"

Emily pushed her forehead into his chest and nodded her head, just once.

"Ah, sweetheart."

Emily felt Matt's lips in her hair and allowed herself to sag against him, knowing he wouldn't let her go. She wound her arms around his trim waist, then flattened her palms against his back. "I've been so scared, Matt."

"And for that, I could rip Morris's spine out," Matt told her, his words low but vicious.

Emily pulled back and looked up into his frustrated face. "You can't tell anybody and you can't confront Nico."

"The hell I can't."

Emily stepped away from him, twisting the material of his shirt in her fist. "Matt, no! I told you because, well…anyway, you cannot do or say anything that will cause Nico to act hastily. Because no matter what you do or say, what I do or say, he will release the photograph and he will start a rumor. It doesn't matter whether it's true or not—it's the perception that counts and he'll spin a damn good story and while we try to fight it, our clients will leave. Nobody else knows about this, well, Gina does, but no one else. Promise me you won't be the one to let the cat out of the bag."

Matt stared at her, the muscle ticking in his jaw. Emily grabbed his biceps and tried to shake him but, because he outweighed her, didn't manage to move him an inch. "Matt! Promise me!"

Matt looked away and when his eyes finally reconnected with hers, she saw that his anger had faded and that some measure of thoughtfulness had returned. He exhaled and rubbed his hands over his face. "What are you going to do?" he eventually asked.

Emily released a long, relieved sigh. "Frankly, I need dirt on him. Something I can blackmail him with. It's not a pretty solution but it's the cleanest. I thought that maybe you would have something on him, seeing that you worked together years ago."

Matt shook his head. "He's a prick but I don't know of anything that will persuade him to back off."

Emily's heart sank to her toes. She'd been relying on Matt to give her something, anything, but it seemed she was back at square one.

Matt slid his hand around the back of her neck and rested his forehead against hers.

"Don't look like that." He brushed his lips across hers. "We'll find a way to get you out of this because, one thing is for damn sure, you are not marrying that loser."

His words were music to her ears.

"Now come back to bed," Matt told her, gently pulling the ties to her gown open. "It's a new day and I can't think of a better way to start it than by making love to you."

"Got a minute, Em?"

Emily looked from her computer monitor to the door and waved Gina in. She closed down her untouched spreadsheet and pushed her chair back from her desk, thinking that she really needed to do some work at some point. But since Matt left her bed early yesterday morning, she'd been less than useless, her thoughts jumping between horrified shock that she'd told him she was being blackmailed into marriage and shivery shock at the way he made her body vibrate with pleasure.

He'd kissed her from top to toe, and she'd loved every second being naked with him. The man had su-

perior bedroom skills and yep, he'd had her screaming with pleasure.

And, better than that, some of her skills had Matt
groaning and growling her name!

"Whoo boy, I want whatever you are having," Gina
said, sitting down in the chair opposite her and cross-
ing her shapely legs.

Emily opened her mouth to tell Gina that she'd
slept with Matt but, at the last minute, she hauled the
words back, thinking that she wanted to keep him to
herself, just for a little while longer. He was like dis-
covering a long-awaited gift in the back of her closet
and she didn't want to share the surprise, not just yet.

Besides, if—when—their relationship blew up,
because relationships always did, she wouldn't have
to give Gina any explanations.

"Your father is asking for the Morales spreadsheet," Gina told her, glancing down at her notepad.

Emily winced. "It's not ready yet."

"Okay. Have you reconciled the Sheppard bank
accounts?"

Emily grimaced and shook her head. Gina arched
her eyebrows when Emily answered in the negative
to her question. "Have you done any work the past
two days?"

"Not really, no."

Gina smacked her notepad against the edge of Emily's desk. "Well, I'm not sending your dad that email.
You can explain."

Emily nodded meekly, not looking forward to that
confrontation. Her dad was a hard taskmaster and

being his daughter wouldn't exempt her from a why-are-you-behind-in-your-work dressing-down.

Gina folded her arms and tapped her index fingers against her biceps, a sure sign that she was feeling anxious. Emily instinctively knew that she didn't want to hear what Gina had to say and pushed her spine into the back of her chair. She considered excusing herself to go to the bathroom but knew that when she returned, Gina would be waiting for her.

Hell, if Gina really needed to get her point across, she'd paint the letters in the sky if she had to.

"What is it?" Emily asked.

Gina hesitated, something she never did, and Emily's stomach dropped like a stone. "You know that I've been trying to dig up something on Nico, looking for a way to get you out of your engagement?"

Emily nodded. "Did you find something?"

"Nothing that would help you with Nico but I did hear about what he was like when he was working at MJR Investing. Unfortunately, I also heard a lot about Matt, as well."

Emily gripped her hands together, fighting the urge to get up and walk away. She wanted to hear bad news about Nico but she didn't need to hear anything negative about the man she'd given her body to, the man she might be in love with.

Might be? Nope, she was pretty sure she'd taken that fatalistic step into love already.

"Do you want to know what I heard?" Gina quietly asked her.

No, but she had to. She couldn't, as much as she

wanted to, shove her head in the sand. Emily rolled her finger in a silent gesture for Gina to continue. "Nico and Matt worked together, as you know. They both started off as traders on the floor at MJR, both, apparently, quite talented."

"Where did you get this information? And is it credible?" Emily demanded.

"From a trader who worked with both of them. He gave me the name of someone else who also worked at MJR around the same time as Nico did and their stories were remarkably similar. Neither of them had a beef with either Matt or Nico."

So, it wasn't information that could be so easily dismissed. Dammit. "Go on," Emily told Gina.

"Matt and Nico were intense rivals and constantly butted heads. If Matt got a new car, Nico got one better. If Nico took a risk on a trade, Matt took an even greater risk. Everything was a competition, nothing was sacrosanct. They were obsessed with beating each other. And when Matt was promoted to CEO, Nico resigned shortly after."

Emily felt acid burning a hole in her stomach lining. "You didn't mention if they competed over women."

Gina winced. "Yeah, they did, all the time. Not over individual women, nobody mentioned that, but someone did say that if Nico dated a model then Matt would date a supermodel. There were office betting pools around who would bring the sexiest date to office functions."

"Charming," Emily said, feeling ghostly hands

squeezing her throat. She stared down at her shaking hands and forced herself to ask the question. "Do you think it's coincidence that Matt came back into my life right at the time I got engaged to Nico?"

Gina grimaced. "I don't know, Em, only he can answer that. I'm just telling you what I heard so that you have all the facts."

Gina stood and picked up her notebook, tapping it against her thigh. "Look, everyone I've spoken to has told me that Matt is super competitive, he wants what he wants and he doesn't let anything get in his way. He's incredibly focused but, as I was told, when he achieves his goal he often loses interest in what he was pursuing."

"So, he's only interested in me because Nico has something he doesn't," Emily quietly stated.

Gina threw up her hands. "I don't know! I don't want to believe that but neither do I want you falling for Matt and having him discard you when he's bored. And I swear, if he does that, I'll freaking break his knees."

Emily watched Gina leave and after the door closed behind her, rested her forehead on her desk, trying to push away the emotions threatening to overwhelm her so that she could think. Taking a couple of deep breaths, she examined the facts. Matt rejected her years ago on the flimsy excuse that she was too young and drunk. He avoided her for years and, when they did cross paths, they didn't, as per normal, exchange more than a terse greeting. Then, out of the blue, and on the very same night he discovered she was engaged to Nico, Matt pushed his way into her life and into her heart.

He'd gotten her to open up about Nico and Emily couldn't understand why. Was it because of his competitive streak and he wanted what Nico had—her?—or was he genuinely concerned about her predicament?

Emily didn't know and she didn't care. All she knew for sure was that Matt would, eventually, bail out, just like everybody else did. When he got whatever he needed from her—edging Nico out, taking what he had, sex, a boost to his ego—he'd leave her swinging in the wind.

Just like her mom did physically and her dad did mentally.

God, she was such an idiot! She had told herself time and time again not to trust him, not to rely on him, not to open up to him, but she'd failed. And failed spectacularly.

She'd fallen in love with the man, something she'd promised herself she'd never do. Because love had no staying power...she *knew* this.

She had to stop seeing Matt, that was obvious. While she still had most of her heart intact, while she could still function, she had to cut the ties between them.

And hopefully in a few months, in a year, she would've forgotten how he smelled, how his eyes could switch from humorous to intense in a second, how solid and wonderful he felt under her lips and hands. In a year's time she would be laughing about this, mocking herself because she thought herself to be in love…

Twelve months, three hundred and sixty-five days.

In the future, she'd want to smack herself for being such a naive idiot but, right now, all she wanted to do was cry.

So she did, hot, acidic tears that did nothing to soothe the ache in her soul.

It was eight by the time she left the office and Emily, not having gotten much sleep last night, was beyond exhausted, and the crying jag she'd succumbed to earlier made her feel dried out and shattered.

Her soul was tired…

From the depths of her bag she heard her phone ringing but didn't bother to dig it out. She had no desire to talk to Nico and if it was Matt, well, she hadn't answered his other five calls or responded to his slew of text messages, and she didn't want to talk to him now.

She just wanted some peace, something she hadn't experienced for the longest while. Emily pulled her key from the side pocket of her bag and walked across the empty parking lot, tempted to book into a hotel for the night; neither Matt nor Nico would find her there.

She just wanted one night to herself, for herself, to gather her strength and marshal her resources. A bottle of wine, a bubble bath, watching a romantic movie on TV with Fatty and no chance of being interrupted…

"Em—"

Emily yelped and whirled around. She slapped her hand on her heart to keep it from springing from her chest and bent over to catch her breath. She felt Matt's hand on her back. "Sorry, sweetheart, I didn't mean to scare you."

"Holy crap, Velez! What the hell?" Emily yelled.

Matt grimaced and lifted his hands. "Sorry, but you really should pay better attention to your surroundings."

He was lecturing her when he snuck up on her? Taking a deep breath, Emily jerked open her car door and threw her bag over the console to the passenger seat.

Whipping around, she closed the door, leaned back against her car and folded her arms, handing Matt a furious scowl. "Why are you here?"

Matt looked puzzled at her virulent retort. "I've been calling you but you didn't answer. Are you okay?"

"What do you think? You scared the hell out of me."

Matt shook his head. "That's not it. Or it's not all of it. What's going on, imp?"

It hurt too much to hear his pet name for her on his lips. "Just go away, Matt. I can't deal with you or anything else tonight."

Matt reached past her to place his hand on her door, effectively preventing her from climbing into the car and driving off. "What is going on?"

When she didn't answer, Matt spoke again. "Do

you regret what happened last night?" Matt demanded, his voice raspy.

Emily didn't immediately reply. She was being blackmailed into marriage; she didn't owe her blackmailer fidelity. But she did regret sleeping with the man who thought of her as a prize to be won and then thrown away.

Emily, hardening her heart and her attitude, tossed her head and narrowed her eyes at him. "I'm surprised to see you here. I thought, having achieved your goal last night, you would be long gone."

"What the hell are you talking about?"

"You've had what Nico wants so you can walk away. Why haven't you?"

Frustration tightened Matt's expression. "You're not making any sense."

Okay, then she'd spell it out for him. "You didn't want anything to do with me six years ago and you'd exchanged no more than a handful of words with me since then. But as soon as you heard that your archrival, your biggest competitor is engaged, to me, you're all over me like a rash?"

Emily saw emotion flicker in his eyes and, at that moment, knew that it was true. He was only with her because he wanted to beat Nico. Up until that moment she'd hoped, prayed, that she was wrong, that she was overanalyzing or projecting, but there was no denying the truth in his eyes.

When he stepped toward her, she held up her hands to warn him to keep his distance. "God, Matt."

"Let me explain."

"What's there to explain?" Emily demanded. "Just answer me this. If I break it off with Nico, will you be there for me? Do we have a chance at something more, something permanent?"

Matt rubbed the back of his neck. "You're upset and I don't think this is the right time to discuss this."

"Just answer the question!" Emily yelled.

"I don't know!" Matt yelled back. "All I know is that I don't *want* to want you, I don't want to *want* more."

Emily stared at him, completely confused. "What does that even mean?"

Matt jammed his hands into the pockets of his pants. He scowled at her, his face and eyes hard, his beautiful mouth thin with displeasure. "Can we stop arguing, please?"

Emily nodded. "Sure, if that's what you want."

"Why do I get the feeling that there's a subtext to your agreement that I'm not getting?"

"Because you aren't a stupid man," Emily haughtily informed him. "So let me spell it out for you. I don't need your help. And the only thing I needed from you, you gave me last night. I wondered what making love to you was like and now I know so… thanks."

Matt's eyes narrowed to slits at her flippancy. "Your acting skills need work."

"As do your hearing skills," Emily snapped back. "I need you to go. Just walk out of my life and keep walking. You did it all those years ago so do me a favor and do it again."

Matt shoved his hands into his hair and scowled at her.

"If I go, I'm going to keep walking. I'm done with begging you to let me in and to allow me to help you."

Emily felt her heart contract, thinking that she was at the end of her rope and it was fraying. "Fine. Just go."

"If I go, I'm not coming back," Matt told her, his words as hard as pebbles being dropped into a shallow puddle of clear water. "If I go, we're done. Do you understand that?"

A tear rolled down her cheek and Emily closed her eyes, hoping to keep the rest behind her eyelids. "I understand."

She heard the whoosh of air Matt released; he sounded like a balloon deflating. Emily turned and opened the door to her vehicle, telling herself that she couldn't turn around, wouldn't allow herself to look into his beloved face, into those deep, luscious eyes. If she did, she'd cave.

Emily heard his footsteps taking him away from her and forced herself to stay where she was, to not call him back. Tears slid down her face.

He was walking out of her life—no, she'd shoved him out of her life—but what he didn't know was that he was leaving with her ripped and shredded heart.

The next day, in his office across town, Matt tried to concentrate on work but it was a disaster from minute one.

He prided himself on being able to multitask, to

juggle a hundred balls in the air, on his exceptional memory but today his normally agile brain had shut down, his entire attention on Emily's scared eyes, hunched shoulders, the tears rolling down her cheeks.

Matt pushed his shoulders back and rubbed his eyes with his thumbs. *You can't blame anyone else but yourself for this mess you're in, dude—you did everything she accused you of.*

He'd pushed himself into Em's life because he'd always wanted her and because he hated the idea of Nico having her. It wasn't nice and it wasn't pretty and it most certainly wasn't something he took pride in.

But he'd soon stopped thinking with his pride and ego and started tuning in to her, looking past the beautiful face dominated by those amazing violet-colored eyes. He'd seen her loneliness, her determination to be self-reliant and the hurt she'd pushed down deep. He liked her sharp mind and her sly sense of humor and, God, yes, he adored her body.

She was the one woman he could see himself with for the rest of his life. His first reaction, the one he'd had so long ago with images of her as his bride and the mother of his children, was right. And because he was young and stupid, he'd run as fast and as far as he could from her.

He loved her and the thought of her marrying anyone else but him was the equivalent of a tooth abscess, a knife plunged into his heart, a cancer in his stomach.

But her pride was hurt; she thought he was only

with her because of his old rivalry—and it was old and so very dead—with Morris. But, because both he and Morris had been immature, arrogant pricks, their legend lived on and Emily had somehow gotten to hear about their embarrassing interactions.

Man, he'd been such an ass.

The only thing I needed from you, you gave me last night. I wondered what making love to you was like and now I know so...thanks.

Matt rubbed his temples with the tips of his fingers, wondering if she really meant what she'd said. Last night, while making love to her, and because he'd had enough sexual encounters to understand the difference between sex with and without love, he'd thought they had an intense connection, a real meeting of minds and bodies and emotions. He needed to wake up with her, go to sleep with her, hear her laugh, make her smile, explore her body and plumb the depths of her agile mind. He yearned for her to be at the center of the family he now so desperately longed for, to be the mother of the children he suddenly craved.

He'd thought they were on the same page but her words last night made him doubt what he thought they had.

And why hadn't he been able to answer her when she demanded to know what he wanted from her? Because the words *marriage* and *babies* and *forever* had never passed his lips before? Because he was scared? Because he was a coward?

All of the above and more.

Matt leaned back in his chair, conscious of the headache behind his eyes. He swiveled around in his seat and stared out his window at the view of the Hudson River. Emily might think that they were over, and they might be, but whatever was going on with Emily was coming to a head; he knew that like he knew his own signature. And, he didn't care whether she wanted his help or not; he was not stepping out of the ring when she needed him the most.

After Nico was out of her life, she could tell him to go to hell but, until then, he was going to help her, whether she wanted him to or not. And that meant getting to work...

Happy to have something else to focus on besides his hurting heart, Matt turned his focus on how to end Morris.

Killing him sounded good but Matt wasn't keen on a lengthy jail sentence, so he'd have to settle for destroying his reputation. Getting Morris out of Emily's life was all that mattered. After Emily was safe, he'd walk away again because he was damned if he'd stick around where he wasn't wanted. He'd done that when he was young—he hadn't had a choice when it came to his family—but he refused to do that again.

He could patch up his aching heart later; right now he needed to take action to boot Morris out of Em's life. He could, maybe, live without her but he absolutely could not live without knowing she was safe. And, until Morris was away from her, she would never be.

But, dammit, he had no idea how to do that.

Matt looked up as Vee entered his office, holding his favorite mug in her right hand and papers in her left. Matt took his coffee with a grateful smile, sipped and closed his eyes. "Thanks, I needed this."

"You look like hell," Vee commented, placing her papers to the side of his computer.

"I feel like hell," Matt told Vee.

Vee sat down on the edge of the visitor's chair, her normally stern face reflecting her deep concern. "How can I help, Matt?"

"A friend of mine—"

"Emily Arnott—"

Of course Vee knew whom he was referring to; she was crazy intuitive. Or nosy. "—has somehow gotten herself tangled up with Nico Morris."

"The Nico Morris who worked here?" Vee asked, wrinkling her nose.

"Yep. Him."

"I never liked him and he always cut corners. Some of his trades were borderline unethical."

His interest caught, Matt sat up straight. "Really?"

Vee nodded. "At the time of his resignation, I was toying with coming to you about my suspicions, but then he resigned and he wasn't a problem anymore."

Matt grimaced. "I wish you had. I might have something to work with today."

Vee's smile reached her eyes and turned her from plain to pretty. "Well, I did do something that might be considered a little unethical myself…"

Oh, *interesting*. "What did you do?"

"On the day you were promoted to CEO, I worked

late. I had a feeling he was going to leave. I was concerned he'd destroy sensitive company information so I did a backup of his desktop."

Matt pulled his keyboard toward him and quickly checked the company server, identified the files that came from Morris's machine and shook his head. "I've checked these files already. There's nothing there."

Vee stood up, walked around his desk and peered at the screen. "That's a backup done by someone from the IT department. That file is a lot smaller than the one I did two nights before he resigned."

Matt's heart started to gallop and the moisture from his mouth disappeared. "Please, please tell me that you still have that backup."

Vee rolled her eyes. "I file everything. Of course I have it." Vee nudged him aside and Matt rolled his chair back to give Vee access to his keyboard. A minute later she was on the internet and code was rolling across his screen. And then, thirty seconds later, a folder popped up on his home screen, dated five years back.

Vee stood back, gestured to the folder and smiled. "If you find anything worthwhile can I have a raise?"

Matt rolled his chair closer to the desk. "Even if I don't, you can still have a raise," Matt told her, opening the folder and scanning the directory. There was a huge discrepancy in the size between the files he had access to and Vee's backup copy. The obvious place to start was to see what Morris deleted before the techies from IT came in to back up his system.

Matt prayed he would find something he could use.

Ten

Pack a bag, we're heading to Vegas. You'll also need a wedding dress.

Emily read the text message from Nico again and tasted bile in the back of her throat. God, this was happening, this was *really* happening.

So, was this what all those French aristocrats felt like when they were facing the sharp blade of the guillotine? Terrified and subdued, resigned and a little dead on the inside?

Maybe that was the trick to survive the next however many years of marriage to Nico? Don't feel, don't react, don't think.

Just be…

Emily rested her aching head on her office window, feeling utterly wiped out. If she felt like a shell of the person she usually was right now, then there would be nothing left of herself when, and if, she was finally free of Nico.

She couldn't do it.

Emily turned and put her back to the window, her hands flat against the glass. Yes, she'd be taking a huge gamble with the company, with their clients, but they had the financial records to back up every transaction they'd made; their paper trail was clean. Yes, they'd take a hit reputationwise but it wasn't like they'd be going up against a choirboy or the most well-respected person in Falling Brook. Nico wasn't well liked and she and her dad were; maybe they'd have a fighting chance.

She couldn't marry Nico. And she'd rather do battle in the open than skulk in the shadows.

And maybe, just maybe, Matt would help her. Okay, she accepted that she'd never have a happy-ever-after with him but maybe his competitive streak was strong enough to want to take Nico down, to help her. Maybe, possibly, his offer of help was still on the table.

It wasn't like she had any choices left and she'd definitely run out of time. She had to put her pride aside and accept she couldn't do this on her own; she needed help. Matt's help.

Before she could talk herself out of her decision, Emily lunged for her phone and dialed Matt's number, then cursed when it went straight to voice mail.

She didn't bother with a long explanation when a few words would do...

"I know you're mad at me but Nico wants us to leave for Vegas tonight to get hitched. I'm out of my depth and I need your help. Will you help me?"

How long would it take for him to listen to her message? Did she have that much time? Emily bit her lip and placed her hand on her stomach, pushing her other fist into her sternum, trying to ease the burning sensation.

While she waited for Matt to call back, she needed to do what she could to mitigate the disaster looming in her future. And the first step was to confront her father and to make him listen to her. She needed to connect with him, not as employee and boss but as father and daughter.

She needed her *dad*.

Clutching her phone to her chest, Emily walked out of her office and after passing Gina's empty desk, she walked down the hallway to her dad's office. She was going to have to tell him what was going on, inform him of the fight they were about to wade into. She needed to prepare him, to shore up his emotional defenses, to reassure him they would, with Matt's help, be okay. That the business would survive.

That he, and his reputation, would be fine...

Emily knocked, entered and jerked to a stop when she saw Nico lounging in the visitor's chair across from her father. Her dad's eyes looked haunted. His face was the color of fresh, falling snow.

Oh, shit. He already knew.

Even from across the room, Emily could see his trembling chin and lips and the bulging cords in his too-tense neck.

"Emily…"

His voice sounded thin, as if he couldn't get enough air. "Em, what are we going to do? I can't lose the business. I can't. It's all I have."

Emily wanted to scream at him that he had her and Davy, that they were more important than the business, but the words got lodged in her throat.

Emily felt her heart sink and cursed herself for imagining, just for one second, that he'd have a plan, that he'd step up to the plate and find a solution instead of looking to her for one. That he'd put her first, that he'd risk losing his business to save her.

But that wasn't the way her family worked; she made the sacrifices for everyone else.

"I've shown your father the photograph and the press release I intend to send to the police and the press if you don't agree to marry me, in Vegas, tonight. They are pretty damning." Nico sent her a cold smile. "And don't think that Matt Velez is going to ride in on his white horse and rescue you, Emily—he's only interested in you because I have you."

He had her? Who used words like that anymore? God, she couldn't do this, she couldn't tie herself to a misogynistic narcissist. Not for her dad, not to save their reputation…

Her father cleared his throat and she turned her

eyes back to him. "Emily, it's everything I've worked for, all that I have. I won't be able to rebuild the company if our clients leave—the stain on our reputation will be too damaging. I have some savings but I won't be able to keep Davy in Brook Village for more than a few months and even if we both get other jobs, we wouldn't be able to afford the fees. That's even if I manage to find a job because I'm pretty sure I'll slide back into that dark place I was in after your mother left."

Emily knew, from a place far, far away, that this was another type of blackmail but it was working, dammit. She didn't want Davy to leave Brook Village or for her dad to take to his room for months and months. A part of her wanted to scream *what about me?*

But her dad didn't care. The truth was that he didn't want the situation to change and she was the sacrificial goat. But, as much as she wanted to protest, he was right in one aspect: if she refused to marry Nico, Davy would suffer and, of all of them, he was utterly blameless.

Emily knew that she'd run out of choices so she forced the words through her tight throat. "Well, I guess I'm getting married."

Nico slowly climbed to his feet, a smile touching his thin lips. "Excellent." He leaned across Leonard's desk and picked up the photograph and copy of his press release. "Next stop, Vegas."

No, next stop…hell.

* * *

Matt, Emily's left Falling Brook and has gone to Vegas, to get married. What the hell are you going to do about it?

Matt exited the taxi and stepped onto the sidewalk, looking down the busy Vegas Strip, Gina's message bouncing around his head. In between hearing Em's desperate words—*will you help me?*—played over and over again, he kept recounting his less-than-wonderful confrontation with Emily's father hours before. It was a hell of way to start a relationship with your future father-in-law (if all went well) by yelling at him.

Once I calmed down, I tried to call her back, Leonard told him, wringing his hands, his eyes watery with tears. *I reacted badly—I was scared—and I want her to know that she mustn't marry Morris, that we'll fight this but she's not answering her phone.*

Matt climbed out of his taxi and glanced down at his phone, willing it to ring. But the only new message on his screen was one from Leonard, asking for an update. Matt frowned, feeling sick to his stomach. He didn't have an update for anyone; Emily's phone was off, as was Morris's, and he had no idea where to start looking for Emily in Vegas, heaving with tourists. Looking for her in a wedding chapel might yield some results but there were over fifty chapels in the city and he didn't know where to start.

Matt gripped the bridge of his nose between his thumb and index finger and, for the first time in forever, prayed that he would find Emily before she hitched herself to that POS. If he only found her after they were married, well, then he'd get his lawyers working on how to get the marriage annulled or a quickie divorce, but one thing he was crystal clear: Emily would not remain married to Morris.

He might not be able to save Arnott's reputation but he sure as hell could save Emily. If, after fighting back with an intense PR campaign and having one-on-one meetings with every client of Arnott's, they still lost the company and their reputation, he was wealthy enough to keep Davy in Brook Village and to support her dad.

He didn't care about the money: Emily was all that he could think about.

Matt still didn't know if she loved him—she'd asked for his help but hadn't said anything else—and, frankly, it didn't matter. He loved her; she was all that was important. Her happiness, her security, was his ultimate goal; she was his to protect. His heart was hers, whether she wanted it or not.

But to move on, he had to find her! And God, how was he going to do that in a city of more than three million, excluding the tourists?

Matt felt the vibration of his phone and had it to his ear before it could ring. "Vee, anything?"

"I went back through his expense reports from when he was at MJR, padded I'll have you know, and on them I found three payments to the same hotel. I also found more receipts from a bar within the hotel—it's all I could find."

It was, at least, a place to start. And hopefully Nico

was a creature of habit and had returned to the hotel he was familiar with.

"I've sent you the address of the hotel," Vee told him and Matt heard the ping of an incoming message.

"Are there any wedding chapels close to the hotel?" Matt asked, opening her message. He quickly plugged the address into his mapping app and tried to get his bearings. He switched his phone on to loudspeaker as he squinted at the map. It wasn't, thank God, far away.

Matt heard Vee typing and held his breath, waiting for her answer. "Yeah, there's one, just around the corner from the entrance of the hotel."

Matt grinned. "Thanks, Vee, you are an angel."

"I am very much not but that description certainly fits Emily Arnott."

Matt turned around and started heading north, thinking it was quicker to walk than take a taxi in the heavily congested traffic. "She hates being called angelic and it really doesn't suit her. She's obstinate and feisty and too independent by half."

"But you still love her."

He did. "I do. And I always will."

"Then I suggest you run not walk, Matteo Velez."

That was a damn good idea. Matt tucked his phone into the back pocket of his pants and started to sprint, refusing to consider what he'd do if she wasn't in the chapel, if they weren't registered at the hotel.

He would find her because losing her wasn't an option.

* * *

Emily, dressed in a stupid white lace dress Nico insisted they buy at the hotel boutique, sat on the pew in the surprisingly pretty chapel and stared at her shaking hands. The synthetic smell wafting from the fake floral bouquets dotted around the chapel made her want to throw up and a headache threatened to split her head apart.

Could her day possibly get any worse?

Emily stared down at her hands, wishing she was carrying her phone instead of this stupid bunch of white roses. But Nico, jerk that he was, had confiscated her phone and she had no idea where it was. Besides, who should she call? She'd left a message with Matt but she doubted he'd gotten it; she assumed that he seldom checked his phone at work because he was busy running MJR Investing. Her dad? Well, he'd made it very clear that the company and its reputation, and his mental health, were more important than her happiness. Her mom? Funny.

Emily untied the ribbon wound around the stems of the bouquet, allowing the silk to flow between her fingers. It was a pretty bouquet but it represented fear, stress and anguish. Emily ran her finger over the soft petal of the center rose, before methodically stripping the rose of everything that made it luscious and lovely. With every petal that fell, Emily felt like she was losing a little bit of herself, and when the rose was denuded, she promised herself she'd never wear white again.

Ever.

God, what was she going to do? Emily allowed
the last of the petals to flutter to the floor and, dropping the bouquet, wrapped her arms around her waist,
gently rocking back and forth. She was so tired, emotionally whipped and, for the first time since she was
fourteen, ready to give up.

Emily watched a tear plop onto the toe of her shoe,
then another. She didn't bother trying to curtail her
tears; she'd earned her right to bawl her eyes out.

Everything was ruined...

Emily heard the door to the chapel open and, not
bothering to turn around, thought she should vacate
the room; the happy couple walking in wouldn't want
their marriage ceremony to be witnessed by a weepy
woman with a mangled bouquet and a bleak outlook
on marriage.

She wanted to leave, she did, but her legs and arms
were heavy, and she was dreading the future. Emily
slammed her eyes shut, thinking that she just wanted
to stay here for the next few minutes, hours, maybe
for the rest of her life.

"Okay, you're married. Don't panic—we can sort
this out."

Emily opened her eyes to see Matt sitting down
beside her on the pew, his normally olive skin pale
in the subdued light of the chapel. Emily looked into
his luscious eyes and read worry and concern within
those dark depths.

Matt took her trembling hands and lifted both sets
of knuckles to his lips. "I'll sort this out, Em, I will.
You can ask for an annulment, file for divorce—I've

already briefed my lawyers and they are waiting for your call."

Emily, not able to believe that he was here, stared at him, unable to get her brain to work. "Matt? How did you find me?"

"I'll explain later," Matt told her, looking around. "Where's the dipstick?"

"Uh…" Emily blinked, trying to get her brain to work, completely nonplussed by Matt's appearance. He looked a little sweaty, completely harassed and very stressed. To Emily, he'd never looked as gorgeous as he did right then.

"Em, concentrate. Where is Morris?" Matt demanded, giving her a little shake.

"Uh, up in the room," Emily replied, lifting her hand to touch his cheek, needing to check that he wasn't a figment of her imagination. "You're really here."

"I'm really here." Matt turned his head to drop a kiss into her palm. "I know that you have had a completely shitty day, sweetheart, but we need to work out the quickest and easiest way to get you out of this marriage."

Emily blinked at him, his words not making sense. She looked down at her bare ring finger of her left hand just to check. "I didn't marry him, Matt."

Matt's mouth dropped open and he stared at her, his face reflecting his confusion. "What?"

Emily lifted her shoulders and dropped them again. "I couldn't do it. I mean, I was going to, up until the preacher started saying love and cherish and in sickness and in health and I just couldn't. I told Nico to take his chances, that I wasn't going to marry him. He lost his temper and started screaming and yelling and then the preacher person told him to leave." Emily bit her bottom lip. "He's probably up in the room, sending the photograph and his press release to news outlets."

A muscle started to tick in Matt's cheek and his eyes turned cold and hard. "How long ago did this happen?"

It felt like years had passed but it couldn't be any more than ten minutes, as Emily informed Matt. "What's the room number?" Matt demanded.

Emily told him and when Matt leaped to his feet, Emily knew that he was headed upstairs. While she appreciated his gesture, there was nothing he could do. Nico, because he was a self-serving, malicious bastard, would've already played his cards. Emily grabbed Matt's arm.

"It's too late. It's over and I have to live with the consequences. We'll be okay, if Arnott's is destroyed. I'll make a plan. I always do."

Matt stared down at her, shaking his head. "Yeah, that's the problem—it's always you trying to make it work, by yourself. I told you that I'd stand in your corner with you—when are you going to realize that you are no longer alone?"

"I'm not?" Emily asked, hope piercing holes in her despair.

Matt dropped a quick, hard kiss on her lips. "No, dammit, you're not. I'm going to go now but I want you to go back to the hotel and wait in the lobby for me—I promise I'll meet you there as soon as I can."

"But…where are you going?" Emily demanded as he started to walk away.

Matt turned and one corner of his mouth lifted. "I'm going to beat the crap out of Morris. I thought that was self-explanatory."

Emily watched Matt stride away and, after a minute of trying to make sense of the last five minutes, jumped up to follow him. She hadn't bailed out of marrying Morris, risking everything she loved to see Matt in jail on assault charges.

And if he did punch Nico, she'd punch him too because if Matt was going to jail, she'd be there beside him. She loved him and they were, apparently, a team. Where he went, so did she.

Those lawyers, she thought, hurrying to catch up to Matt, were going to be working overtime.

Nico opened the door to his room and Matt didn't hesitate, he just grabbed his shirt and flung Morris into the nearest wall. Matt watched as his head bounced off a picture frame and smiled with satisfaction. That had to have hurt.

Surprisingly, Morris came back swinging but Matt ducked, plowed his fist into his sternum and followed that up with another punch to his nose. Nico yelped, covered his face with his hands and Matt used the opportunity to pin Morris to the wall by placing his forearm across his throat.

Nico's pale blue eyes bulged in fear. "What do you want, Velez?"

"Many things, Nico, many things," Matt softly told him, "but top of the list would be seeing your useless ass in jail."

"That's not going to happen," Morris said, with as much certainty as he could.

Matt pushed his arm harder into his throat. "Now, the SEC might feel differently."

"You have no proof!"

Matt raised his eyebrows. "You wiped your desktop before you left MJR but not before Vee did a backup. I have a mile-long list of emails detailing your involvement in insider trading."

Morris's white face turned whiter. He tried to struggle but then he slumped and his knees gave out.

"Matt, please... Don't. Don't send me to jail."

Matt stepped away from him, disgusted by his whining.

"I haven't sent those photos yet, nobody else has seen them but Emily and Leonard," Nico desperately added.

Matt stepped away from Nico and looked around the room, spying Nico's laptop on the desk in the corner.

Matt hurried over to the computer, frowning when he saw his email program. Matt quickly moved the mouse, clicked on the Sent box and scanned the emails he'd recently sent. When he realized that Morris was telling the truth and that nothing had been sent since last night and specifically nothing about Emily, Matt finally pulled in a breath.

Matt glanced over at Nico, saw that he was still struggling for air, his shirt front nicely saturated with blood from his broken nose, and went back to the home screen. He looked for a program, opened it and pulled his phone from his back pocket.

"Vee, here's the number to remote access his laptop," Matt instructed, rattling off the number to give Vee complete access to Morris's computer. "Are you positive you can wipe it clean, including any cloud accounts?"

Matt heard and ignored Morris's mumbled protest and listened to his exceptional assistant instead. "Matteo, have some faith."

Matt stood back and watched as a ghost arrow floated over the screen and then the screen went black, to be replaced with code running across it. While he waited for Vee to run her magic, Matt calmly opened Nico's briefcase and went through his papers, removing anything with reference to Emily and Arnott's, including the hard copies of the photographs and the copy of the press release. He also grabbed Emily's cell phone and tucked it into the back pocket of his pants.

Matt looked over to Nico, who was leaning back against the wall. "Unless you want me to call Sokolov and tell him how you were using him to blackmail Emily, I suggest that you stand up and walk your pitiful ass out of this room. And if I ever see you in

Falling Brook, if I even hear your name, I will find
you and finish what I started. Got it?"

Nico nodded and stood up slowly, covering his
nose with his hand. Matt walked over to him and,
keeping the laptop and the papers he'd found, handed
Nico his briefcase. "Get the hell out of here, Morris,
you worm."

Nico walked slowly to the open door and when he
reached it, Emily flew into the room, nearly knocking
him over. She stopped in her tracks and grimaced.
Matt caught her eye and frowned at her. "I thought I
told you to wait downstairs in the lobby."

Emily narrowed her eyes at him. "I'm not good at
listening to orders."

"I noticed." Matt jerked his head. "Come here,
Em."

He didn't want her anywhere near Morris; the
thought made him want to punch someone, prefera-
bly Morris, again. Emily inched her way around Nico
and hurried across the room to him, then stepped into
his open arms and snuggled in close.

"Close the door behind you, Morris," Matt said,
and when the door clicked shut, Emily tipped her
head up to look at him, her eyes filled with questions.

"Is it done?"

Matt looked down at the completely normal-looking
screen and remembered that Vee was still on the other
side of the open line. He lifted the receiver to his ear.
"Are you finished?"

"Sure am," Vee replied. "I wiped out his cloud
accounts. Please tell me you had the good sense to

confiscate his laptop because nothing is ever completely erased."

"I did."

"Good boy," Vee replied, as if he wasn't in his thirties and she didn't work for him. "Now, sort out your personal life, Matteo."

"Yes, ma'am." Matt disconnected the call and when he looked down at his screen, he saw at least a dozen missed calls from Leonard. He showed Emily the screen and watched a frown appear between her eyes.

"He's worried sick," Matt explained. "He didn't mean to throw you to the wolves—he tried to call you back."

He saw a little of her anguish diminish but a lot of hurt remained. "I can't talk to him just yet, Matt. I need some time."

Matt nodded. "Let me quickly send him a text message so he can stop worrying."

Matt, his arms still around her, typed a quick text to her father before tossing the phone onto the sofa. Gathering her close, he held her tightly, resting his head on her bright hair, thankful to have her in his arms, safe and, yeah, unmarried.

It was over and they could relax.

Matt lifted his hands up to cradle her face and slowly lowered his mouth to hers.

So much had happened today that Emily wasn't sure whether she was coming or going, but Matt's hot kisses and his clever hands on her body she understood. Emily wound her arms around his back, holding on tight, content to follow his lead as he dropped lazy kisses on her lips and along her jaw.

Needing to feel his bare skin under her hands, to ground herself, Emily pulled his shirt out of the back of his pants and slid her hands up and under the fabric, digging her fingertips into his warm, masculine skin. Needing more, she lifted one hand, held his jaw and turned it back so that he could kiss her, giving her the long, deep and drugging kisses she so badly needed.

Nothing about today made sense but being in Matt's arms did.

"Let me love you, imp," Matt murmured the words against her lips. "Let me take you to bed and let me love you with nothing between us."

Em knew what he was saying, that this was a new start for both of them, a blank page. She wasn't Nico's fiancée and they didn't need to hide—they could be who they were, honestly and openly. She wanted that…no, she needed a new start, a fresh beginning.

Emily stepped back and held out her hand to Matt. When his fingers gripped hers, she tugged him toward the bedroom, then opened the door to a huge bed covered in white linen. Through the open drapes she had a view of downtown Las Vegas, but she wasn't interested in what lay outside her window—Matt held all her attention.

Standing next to the bed, Emily turned her back to Matt and pulled her hair off her shoulders. "Unzip me, please—I can't wait to get out of this dress."

Matt eased the zipper down and Emily released her breath when his lips kissed the bumps of her spine. She felt his hands on her shoulders, easing the dress down her arms until it pooled at her feet. Emily kicked it into the corner of the room with the toe of her white stiletto.

Emily tried to turn but his hands on her hips kept her facing forward, and he buried his face in her neck, breathing deeply. "Your scent drives me wild."

Emily smiled—his scent had always done the same to her, as she breathlessly told him.

"I should have taken you up on your offer six years ago, Em—we've wasted so much time."

This wasn't the time for talking, not yet. Right now, she just wanted to feel and to be with this amazing man. Emily spun around and placed her hands on his broad shoulders, looking up into his messy hair and still-shadowed eyes. "Later, we'll talk later. Right now I need you to love me. We need a new start, a fresh start."

Matt nodded before dropping his mouth to cover hers. Bending his knees, he wound his arms around the backs of her thighs and easily boosted her up his body, urging her to encircle his hips with her legs, allowing her shoes to drop to the floor. Emily, only dressed in her bra and panties, pushed her aching breasts into his chest. "You have too many clothes on, Matteo."

"Funny, I was just thinking the same thing about you," Matt replied, his free hand sliding behind her back, quickly unsnapping her bra. Emily leaned back in his arms and pulled the garment off, reveling in the passion in Matt's eyes as he stared down at her chest.

"You are indescribably beautiful, Emily Arnott."

Emily flushed, a little embarrassed, a lot turned on. Matt lifted one breast in his hand, testing her weight, his thumb sliding across her distended nipple. "Lean back," Matt told her and Emily didn't hesitate. She'd trusted him with her Morris situation and he, even though he'd thought they were over, had come to Vegas to help her. She trusted him implicitly, with her heart and her body.

Em leaned back and Matt dipped his head to pull her nipple into his mouth, to swipe his tongue over her, sending prickles of pleasure rocketing through her. He moved to her other breast and lathered it with love, and Emily couldn't keep her moans of encouragement to herself.

Matt lifted his head to look at her, his deep, dark eyes intense. "Don't be afraid to tell me what you like or don't like, imp."

"I really like that," Em told him.

Matt grinned and he suddenly looked ten years younger than he did in the chapel. "Good to know." Matt held her close and allowed her to slide down his body, groaning when the vee of her legs slid over his pipe-hard erection. Emily, because she could, placed the palm of her hand over the bulge in his pants, testing his length and his strength. The first time she saw him she'd noticed, as naive as she was, how masculine he was and if anything, the passing years had made him even more so. A small part of her was glad she hadn't known him at nearly twenty-one; she hadn't been enough of a woman for him then, but now she was.

Emily gently pushed Matt's hands off her and reached for the buttons of his shirt, before slowly sliding them open to reveal his chest. She pushed his shirt off his shoulders, eyeing the bulging muscles in his arms, his hard pecs and gorgeous, ridged stomach. "Love your body, Velez," Emily murmured.

"Love yours more," Matt replied, his voice hoarse. "Can I please touch you now?"

Emily shook her head, smiling. "Not just yet."

Reaching for the band of his pants, she popped open the button, worked his zipper down and pushed his pants down his hips, resting her head on his chest as she looked down at his very impressive package.

He wanted her; she could see it in his eyes, in his pants. Suddenly Emily couldn't wait any longer; she needed him, in her and now. Jerking her head up, she met Matt's eyes, hers gaze open and frank. "Can I ask you one favor?"

"Anything, imp, you know that."

"Can we just strip and can we climb onto that bed and can you drive away the bad memories and replace them with something wonderful and, well, good?"

Matt swiped his mouth across hers, once and then again. "Darling, don't you know that there's nothing I wouldn't do for you?"

Emily shimmied out of her panties and, after taking Matt's hands, placed them between her legs. He instinctively and immediately found her small bundle

of pleasure, sending hot flashes through her. Hovering
on the brink of orgasm, Emily felt Matt pull back and
then he was lifting her onto the bed and a few seconds
later, he was naked and looming over her, his shaft
probing her entrance. Emily wound her legs around
his hips and pushed up, sighing when he filled and
then completed her.

Matt rocked once, then again and Emily shuddered, the cliff she was standing on falling away and
crashing into the sea. She screamed as she plummeted, only to be lifted up again and hurtled toward
the sun. Matt plunged within her, his hoarse voice
urging her to come again and because he asked her to,
she spasmed again as he emptied himself inside her.

As she floated back to reality, Matt heavy and
damp as he lay on her, Em turned her head and smiled
as a beam of sunlight hit the edge of their bed.

Everything, including sex, was better in the bright
light of honesty and freedom.

Eleven

Emily rolled over, slowly opened her eyes and blinked at the clock sitting on the bedside table. Night had fallen and she realized she'd been asleep for three, no, four hours. Rubbing her eyes, she slowly sat up and, feeling a cool breeze hit her skin, realized she was naked.

Emily pulled the bedcovers up to her chest and tucked them under her armpits. She slowly rubbed the bare skin on her ring finger, happy to be rid of the ostentatious, probably fake diamond.

She was also free of Nico; she wasn't in danger of losing Arnott's, and her life, as of this moment, was back to normal.

But what did normal mean? If it meant going back

to a life without Matt in it, she'd pass, thank you very much.

She loved him…and not only because he'd broken Nico's nose. No, she loved him because, despite telling her that he wouldn't, he'd come running when she told him she needed him, when she'd asked him for his help. She loved him because he'd been there for her, because he stood in the ring with her, because he'd waded—figuratively and literally—into her fight.

But she also loved him because, well, he was Matt, and he deserved love. He was funny and caring and tough and determined and loyal and, yeah, sexy.

Matt walked into the room, sat on the bed beside her and tucked a long strand of hair behind her ear. "You're smiling," he commented, his thumb skating over her cheekbone.

Emily's lips twitched. "I was just thinking how sexy you are and how good you make me feel. You wore me out and I passed out."

"While I'm happy you think I'm a stud, I think the fact that you haven't been sleeping well for weeks might've contributed to you falling asleep on my chest." Matt pulled his thigh up on the bed and rested his hand on her knee. "How are you feeling, imp?"

Emily, losing herself in his deep, dark eyes, considered his question. "Good." The tips of her fingers drifted across the top of his hand. "Thank you for coming to help me—I'm so grateful you did."

"Sweetheart, when are you going to realize that there isn't anything I wouldn't do for you? You call and I come—that's the way it works, the way it will always work." He looked at his swollen knuckles and half smiled. "There isn't anyone I wouldn't fight, there's no limit on the amount of money I'll spend, the distance I'll travel…you can ask anything of me, Em."

Could she, really? He looked sincere, sounded genuine and if she didn't ask, she'd never know. "Can I ask you one more favor, Matteo?"

"Sure."

Emily sucked in a deep breath and with it, a blast of courage. "Do you think there's any chance of you standing in the ring with me for the rest of my life? Will you be my person, my rock, the one person I can rely on and trust?"

Matt stroked his hand down her messy hair. A smile danced across his lips. "Yes to all of the above."

Emily let out a shaky laugh. "You didn't even stop to think about that!"

Matt lifted one shoulder in a casual shrug. "I don't need to. I wanted you in my life six years ago but neither of us were ready for each other and when I saw you again, I knew I wanted you in my bed. It wasn't long before I knew I wanted you in my life, although I tried to fight that."

Matt looked down and for the first time she saw him stripped of his confidence. "There are things I've got to say to you, Em, and it's not easy…"

Emily immediately shook her head. "You don't need to. This is a new day and a new start."

Determination flooded Matt's face. "No, honey, we need to do this because if we don't, it'll always be there. We can't move forward until we address the past."

Emily took his hand and held it between her own two.

"I told you, briefly, that my parents were all about Juan. What I failed to mention was that they had absolutely no interest in me, at all."

Emily wanted to say something, anything, but knew he wouldn't appreciate pity and sympathy might cause him to shut down. So she gave him the best gift she could: silence and her complete attention.

"I tried to do everything he could, with no measure of success. No matter what I did, I couldn't be perfect and that was what Juan was, to them. My default mechanism was to compete and when I realized I couldn't, that he was way out of my league, I rebelled. My competitive streak came back when I went to college and realized I could actually win at some things. Then winning became an addiction."

"Okay…"

Matt looked down at their linked fingers. "At the same time I was trying to compete with Juan all I ever wanted was something, anything, from my parents. I gave up wishing for toys or new clothes or a bike for Christmas and started praying for the big things— a kind word, a hug, conversation, affection. But the more I wanted it, the more elusive their attention became. Eventually, I stopped hoping and decided that dreams were for fools and if I didn't want, I couldn't be disappointed."

Wow, their parents had really messed them up,

in different but equally destructive ways. It was a minor miracle that both she and Matt were as normal as they were.

"With you it was the perfect storm."

Emily frowned. "Me?"

The corners of Matt's mouth lifted. "Six years ago, I saw you and I think, at the risk of sounding, cheesy, I recognized you."

"We'd never met before," Emily informed him, puzzled.

"I don't mean it like that—I recognized you as being...*mine*. For the first time since I was a kid, I wanted something, someone, so much that it scared me so I ran. Hard and fast."

Emily leaned forward and dropped a kiss on his bare shoulder and rested her forehead against his collarbone.

"Six years later and I see you again and you're engaged. Worse than that, you're engaged to a man I competed against. I told myself that I was interested in you because I wanted to take you away from him, because I was a competitive douche and I was. But, underneath the lies I was telling myself, because wanting and dreaming and being disappointed wasn't something I was prepared to feel again, I knew what I felt six years ago was still the truth."

Turning her face into Matt's neck, Emily kissed him, once, then again.

"You are what I want and what I need. You are my biggest dream, Emily. Winning has always been important to me, but, with you, I don't care if I don't get all that I want from you. I'll settle for what I can get. So yes, I'll stand in the ring with you."

Matt looked down, bit his lip and Emily was touched to see her alpha man looking vulnerable. And when he lifted his eyes back to hers, she saw the love within those depths, love he'd been needing to give someone and was prepared to offer her. "Do you think you could ever love me?" he asked.

She wouldn't make him beg; that wasn't fair. Nor would she tease him or make him wait. This was too important; he was *all* that was important. "But I do love you, Matt, intensely, crazily. You're..." Emily hesitated, looking for the words to make him understand.

"I'm what?"

"You're what I've been looking for since I was fourteen, the missing piece of my heart. Strong, steady, reliable and God knows, sexy."

The corners of Matt's mouth twitched but his eyes remained serious, as if needing more. She could give him more; there wasn't anything she'd hold back from him. "It feels like I've been on a long, lonely road and when I met you again, it felt like I'd arrived home. You're my home, Matt. You are what the rest of my life looks like."

Happiness replaced the apprehension in his eyes. Emily smoothed the wrinkles out of the sheet covering her knee. "I've been used to operating on my own—"

"And that changes today," Matt interrupted her.

Emily smiled at his very alpha-male, top-dog comment. "And it might take me a while to get used to that but I'll do everything I can to make us work."

Matt shook his head. "I'll make you happy. And I promise to protect you always. I'll make us work—I promise."

Emily slid her hand under his and pushed her fingers between his. "I don't know much about relationships but I'd like to think that, if we decide to jump in—"

"Oh, we're jumping in," Matt insisted.

Emily smiled. "—we go in knowing we're on an equal footing with both of us committed to making each other happy. We won't always both be strong at the same time, Matt—we'll take turns being strong for each other, protecting each other when the other feels weak."

Emily saw a hint of doubt on Matt's face and shook her head. "I've always been the strong one, for my dad and for Davy, but that doesn't mean that I now think that I have to be weak or want to be protected all the time. You've also been alone for a long time and the only way this can work is if we go forward as a team. Can we do that?"

Matt pushed his hand through his hair. "Yes, okay…" Matt hooked a finger in the edge of the blanket and tugged. "Can we stop talking now and can I show you how much I love you?"

"In a minute…" Emily looked out the window, wishing they didn't have to talk about Nico but knowing that they must. They needed to move, permanently, past him.

"Do you think he'll come back to Falling Brook?" Emily asked Matt.

"He'd be stupid if he does," Matt replied. "I sent a dossier to the SEC detailing some of his dodgy trades and I've no doubt that Morris will be investigated. I'm not sure if he'll face a criminal charge. You can also lay charges against him for blackmailing you. Morris is going to have a lot to deal with in the near future." He paused, then added, "And I threatened to tear him from limb to limb if he comes back."

"And the photograph of my dad and Sokolov?"

"I have the hard copies from his briefcase. I very much doubt Morris will resurrect his blackmail attempt. I think that ship has sailed."

Emily mulled over his words, agreeing he was right. "Talking about another aspect of the future, are you going to take the job offer from Black Crescent?"

Matt shook his head. "No, I'm not. I used them to twist my board's arm but also because I have this thing about winning, about wanting to be chosen. Knowing that you love me and that you have chosen me, that's all I need. Besides, Vee isn't keen to move from MJR to Black Crescent."

"And we can't upset Vee," Emily teased.

"Damn straight."

Matt leaned forward and nuzzled her cheek with his lips. "Can I propose a way forward, a plan of action?"

Emily's mouth twitched with amusement. "Certainly."

"I suggest that you drop the blankets and let me love you again. And after that, why don't we head out? I know a small, lovely restaurant and maybe, if I give you enough wine, I can talk you into marrying me, right now, here in Vegas. I can't wait to make you mine, imp," Matt added.

Emily's heart bounced off her ribcage before doing happy somersaults. She pretended to think, drawing out the anticipation. "I have another idea…why don't we make love, then eat, and then you can bring me back here and we can pretend we're on our honeymoon? Then, in a couple of months, we can make it official back home, with Davy and my dad and all our friends as witnesses." Emily wrinkled her nose. "But…"

Matt arched his eyebrows. "But?"

"But I still expect a kick-ass proposal and," she glared at the rumpled lace dress in the corner, "I absolutely refuse to wear white."

Matt grinned, his face open and full of joy. He tugged the bedcovers away and pulled her into his arms. "Now there's a deal I can't refuse. And, I didn't need to blackmail you into doing it."

Emily wound her arms around his neck and brushed his lips with hers. "And what would you have blackmailed me with, Velez?"

"I would've refused to sleep with you."

"Effective, I have to admit," Emily told him, laughing.

Matt captured her mouth in a long, sexy kiss before pulling back and looking in her eyes. "I know. Now, my delicious imp, be quiet and love me."

It was an order she was happy to obey. "I do—I will…forever."

* * *

Matt poured coffee into two mugs and looked out Emily's windows to the forest beyond her father's yard. They'd been bed hopping for three weeks— from her bed here to his bed in his house across town, and occasionally she stayed over in his apartment in Manhattan—and they were both sick of shuffling around.

Matt felt Fatty brush against his legs and leaned down to pick up Em's very rotund cat. "You weigh a ton, dude. I think we need to think about putting you on a diet."

Fatty responded to that suggestion by digging his claws into his arm. Matt rubbed his ears and head, eyeing the boxes scattered around Emily's apartment. Later on today, the movers would be coming to move all her stuff into the old farmhouse they'd purchased on the outskirts of town.

Their new property would be a fresh start, a place that was theirs as opposed to his or hers and he couldn't wait. And, best of all, Emily had finally decided on a wedding date, three months from now.

Matt, desperate to start a family, had asked her to go off the pill and she'd agreed so, with any luck, their firstborn would arrive before their first wedding anniversary. That might raise some eyebrows of the more conservative folk in town but Matt didn't care. He was, after all, the town rebel who'd corrupted their favorite good girl…

Besides, he'd just make them some more money and all sins would be forgiven. Matt grinned. If those same conservatives knew how his fiancée and the future mother of his children blew his mind last night, and this morning, they'd know exactly how bad his imp could be…

And he loved it. He loved her.

"Where's my coffee?"

Matt lowered Fatty to the floor and smiled at the grumpy words drifting down the short hallway to him. Em was not a morning person and only a cup of coffee, or a deep, drugging morning kiss, turned her grumpiness to gratitude.

God, he was lucky. He'd hit the jackpot; Emily, as beautiful on the inside as she was on the outside, loved him and never missed a chance to tell him how much. And, God, the sex just kept getting better and better. Matt glanced at his watch and decided they had enough time for shower sex before the movers arrived.

Matt picked up Em's coffee and was about to turn away when his electronic tablet beeped with a news alert. Swiping his finger across the screen, he stared down, unable to process the words…

"Vernon Lowell Lives! Black Crescent Fugitive Discovered in Remote Caribbean Location."

Well, now wasn't *that* interesting?

* * * * *

Dynasties:
Seven Sins

It takes the betrayal of only one man
to destroy generations.

When a hedge fund hotshot vanishes with billions,
the high-powered families of Falling Brook
are changed forever.

Now seven heirs, shaped by his betrayal,
must reckon with the sins of the past.

Passion may be their only path to redemption.

Experience all Seven Sins!

Ruthless Pride *by Naima Simone*
Forbidden Lust *by Karen Booth*
Insatiable Hunger *by Yahrah St. John*
Hidden Ambition *by Jules Bennett*
Reckless Envy *by Joss Wood*
Untamed Passion *by Cat Schield*
Slow Burn *by Janice Maynard*

Available May through November 2020!

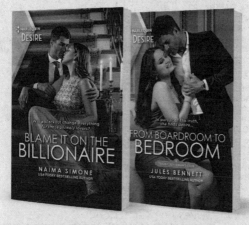

A tempting new music venture reunites songwriter Eden Voss with ex-boyfriend Blaine Woodson, a record label executive. He wronged her in the past, so they vow to keep things strictly business this time. But there is nothing professional about the heat still between them...

Read on for a sneak peek at
After Hours Redemption *by Kianna Alexander.*

Singing through the opening verse, she could feel the smile coming over her face. Singing gave her a special kind of joy, a feeling she didn't get from anything else. There was nothing quite like opening her mouth and letting her voice soar.

She was rounding the second chorus when she noticed Blaine standing in the open door to the booth. Surprised, and a bit embarrassed, she stopped midnote.

His face filled with earnest admiration, he spoke into the awkward silence. "Please, Eden. Don't stop."

Heat flared in her chest, and she could feel it rising into her cheeks. "Blaine, I..."

"It's been so long since I've heard you sing." He took a step closer. "I don't want it to be over yet."

Swallowing her nervousness, she picked up where she'd left off. Now that he was in the room, the lyrics, about a secret romance between two people with plenty of baggage, suddenly seemed much more potent.

And personal.

Suddenly, this song, which she often sang in the shower or while driving, simply because she found it catchy, became almost autobiographical. Under the intense, watchful gaze of the man she'd once loved, every word took on new meaning.

She sang the song to the end, then eased her fingertips away from the keys.

Blaine burst into applause. "You've still got it, Eden."

"Thank you," she said, her tone softer than she'd intended. She looked away, reeling from the intimacy of the moment. Having him as a spectator to her impassioned singing felt too familiar, too reminiscent of a time she'd fought hard to forget.

"I'm not just gassing you up, either." His tone quiet, almost reverent, he took a few slow steps until he was right next to her. "I hear singing all day, every day. But I've never, ever come across another voice like yours."

She sucked in a breath, and his rich, woodsy cologne flooded her senses, threatening to undo her. Blowing the breath out, she struggled to find words to articulate her feelings. "I appreciate the compliment, Blaine. I really do. But…"

"But what?" He watched her intently. "Is something wrong?"

She tucked in her bottom lip. *How can I tell him that being this close to him ruins my concentration? That I can't focus on my work because all I want to do is climb him like a tree?*

"Eden?"

"I'm fine." She shifted on the stool, angling her face away from him in hopes that she might regain some of her faculties. His physical size, combined with his overt masculine energy, seemed to fill the space around her, making the booth feel even smaller than it actually was.

He reached out, his fingertips brushing lightly over her bare shoulder. "Are you sure?"

She trembled, reacting to the tingling sensation brought on by his electric touch. For a moment, she wanted him to continue, wanted to feel his kiss. Soon, though, common sense took over, and she shook her head. "Yes, Blaine. I'm positive."

Will Eden be able to maintain her resolve?

Don't miss what happens next in…
After Hours Redemption *by Kianna Alexander.*

Available October 2020 wherever
Harlequin Desire books and ebooks are sold.

Harlequin.com

HDEXP0920

From acclaimed author

ADRIANA HERRERA

Starting over is more about who you're with than where you live…

Running the charitable foundation of one of the most iconic high fashion department stores in the world is serious #lifegoals for ex–New Yorker Julia del Mar Ortiz, so she's determined to stick it out in Dallas—despite the efforts of the blue-eyed, smart-mouthed consultant who intends to put her job on the chopping block.

When Julia is tasked with making sure Rocco sees how valuable the programs she runs are, she's caught between a rock and a very hard set of abs. Because Rocco Quinn is almost impossible to hate—and even harder to resist.

"Herrera excels at creating the kind of rich emotional connections between her protagonists that romance readers will find irresistible." —*Booklist* on *American Dreamer*

Order your copy now!

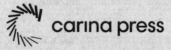

carina press

CarinaPress.com

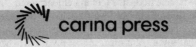
He brought his cat to dinner.

I opened the door to my apartment and found Rocco holding the
little carrier we'd bought for Pulga at the pet store in one hand and
in the other he had a reusable shopping bag with what looked like
his contribution for dinner.

"Hey, I know you said she was uninvited." His eyebrows
dipped, obviously worried I'd be pissed at this plus-one situation.
I wanted to kiss him so bad, I was dizzy. "But whenever I tried to
leave the house, she started mewling really loud. I think she's still
dehydrated."

Boy, was I in over my head.

I smiled and tried not to let him see how his words had actually
turned me into a puddle of goo. "It's fine, since she's convalescent

and all, but once she's back in shape, she's banned from this apartment."

He gave a terse nod, still looking embarrassed. "Promise."

I waved him on, but before I could get another word in, my mom came out of my room in full "Dia de Fiesta" hair and makeup. Holidays that involved a meal meant my mother had to look like she was going to a red carpet somewhere. She was wearing an orange sheath dress with her long brown hair cascading over her shoulders and three-inch heels on her feet.

To have dinner in my cramped two-bedroom apartment.

"Rocco, you're here. *Qué bueno.*" She leaned over and kissed him on the cheek, then gestured toward the living room. "Julita, I'm so glad you invited him. We have too much food."

"Thank you for letting me join you." Rocco gave me the look that I'd been getting from my friends my entire life, that said, *Damn, your mom is hot.* It was not easy to shine whenever my mother was around, but we were still obligated to try.

I'd complied with a dark green wrap dress and a little bit of mascara and lip stain, but I was nowhere near as made-up as she was. Except now I wished I'd made more of an effort, and why was I comparing myself to my mom and why did I care what Rocco thought?

I was about to say something, anything, to get myself out of this mindfucky headspace when he walked into my living room and, as he'd done with my mom, bent his head and brushed a kiss against my cheek. As he pulled back, he looked at me appreciatively, his gaze caressing me from head to toe.

"You look beautiful." There was fluttering occurring inside me again, and for a second I really wished I could just push up and kiss him. Or punch him. God, I was a mess.

Don't miss what happens next…
Here to Stay *by Adriana Herrera*
available wherever Carina Press books
and ebooks are sold.

CarinaPress.com